John B Spencer

lives in west London with his wife and the youngest of their three sons. This is his fourth novel, and the third in the Charley Case series. He is also a highly-respected songwriter and musician and has released a number of CDs.

Quake City

A NOVEL BY
JOHN B SPENCER

BLOODLINES

First Published in Great Britain in 1996 by
The Do-Not Press
PO Box 4215
London SE23 2QD

A Paperback Original

Copyright © 1996 by John B Spencer
All rights reserved

ISBN 1 899344 02 0

British Library Cataloguing in Publication Data. A catalogue record for this book is available from the British Library.

All rights reserved. No part of this publication may be reproduced, transmitted or stored in a retrieval system, in any form or by any means without the express permission in writing of The Do-Not Press having first been obtained.

This book is sold on the condition that it shall not, by way of trade or otherwise, be lent, resold or hired out or otherwise circulated without the publisher's prior consent in any form of binding or cover other than that in which it is published and without a similar condition being imposed on the subsequent purchaser.

Printed and bound in Great Britain by The Guernsey Press Co Ltd, Guernsey, Channel Islands

Dedicated to The O'Dufferty's...
including the male child.

Authors Note:
When the Big One of Ninety-Seven opened up Valencia Gap and created the Nevada Sea, California had picked itself up, dusted itself down, and started all over again. Even before the mammoth task of rebuilding had begun, the Californians, a conservative people by nature, had elected to stick with all the original street names. The consequence of this is that any specific locations referred to in this Charley Case novel don't necessarily relate to their counterparts in twentieth century California.

Have a nice day!

Chapter One

If I hadn't had a falling out with Hetty O'Hara that last night in March at the Top Button Diner on Main Street, Santa Monica, maybe the dice wouldn't have fallen the way they did. Maybe, when Ross Helgstrom put in his call at that crazy time of eight-thirty the following morning, I'd have climbed halfway out of sweet-dream land, traced Hetty's warm contours beside me in the bed, burrowed my stubble into the soft tangle of her auburn hair, and left the phone to ring.

Maybe...

But when you pass the dice, you pass the dice. Nobody in this world gets a chance to see what they might have thrown. Especially, a nobody like me. A nobody with more big mistakes locked away in his junk-heap of a metal filing cabinet than there are cracked-up hang-gliders nesting in the conifers on the fast slopes of the High Sierras.

Sure, I could blame Hetty.

Blame her for the clone-bred clams, and the sea bass that tasted like some wino had found it stranded on the Santa Monica beach at low tide, given it to the cook in exchange for a bottle of house vino rock-bottom.

Blame her for having the kind of friends who could recommend a dump like the Top Button.

Blame her for the lousy mood I was in by the time she came on with the let's keep it uncomplicated, Charley, routine... good friends, mature enough to make out without it all getting out of hand.

'What do you say, Charley?'

I had plenty to say, and none of it the right thing. By the time the kid in the white tuxedo and scuffed sneakers came by with the sweet trolley, nobody was buying...

Period.

Hetty O'Hara had just been promoted from Community Relations Officer to Detective Second Grade working out of the West Hollywood Precinct House. We were supposed to be out celebrating. My line of work, I've been around detectives first, second and tenth grade. The difference was I had never fallen for one of them before.

Sure, I could blame Hetty.

Why the hell not?

After the row, after Hetty had stormed out of the restaurant, I settled for a bottle of lukewarm tequila, scored a couple of cheap points against the kid who had served us, and drove back to my apartment in Century City.

Ross Helgstrom's call next morning found me on the sofa. I had a head full of yesterday's refrieds and a stale *taco* shell where my tongue used to be. Ten floors below I could hear the build of commuter traffic making fast time through the low profile patrolled streets of Century City, burning Plentygas like there was still something left to prove to the Arab Nations. As I moved to grab the receiver the refrieds slopped around some.

I should have guessed it wasn't Hetty.

Should have known that when you're in love, you get to be everybody's April Fool.

I unglued the receiver but remained silent.

'Charley Case?'

The voice asking the difficult questions was young, West Coast, male.

'I'll pass on that one.'

'Did I wake you?'

'Not yet.'

'You were recommended by a mutual acquaintance, Hogie Corcoran.'

That didn't make the recommendation reciprocal. Hogie Corcoran was a barfly who kept a stool warm down at Soaks, on Washington. A small-time hustler with three shells but no pea to shuffle. Two hundred and fifty pounds of raw meat with a face like an avalanche in motion, who hired out as muscle to bottom-line his hard liquor habit. Anybody tells you there are no grizzlies left in the State of California, except on the state flag and in the zoo, tell them go see Hogie.

'You still there?'

'That's another pass.'

'If I say I have a job you can do for me, small service, good money, will that get a response?'

'Depends.'

'You're not making this easy.'

'It's eight-thirty a.m., last night I had a row with my best girl, I'm hung-over and feel like shit. Why should I make it easy?'

'Put like that...'

'You could start in by telling me who it is I'm talking to.'

'So, okay. I started this all wrong...right? I'm sorry. I should have known you just fell out with your significant other. I should have known you went on the drunk last night and that eight-thirty a.m. was the wrong time to be calling — only, I have a nine-fifteen shuttle to make and I'm way behind schedule. My name is Ross Helgstrom, I'm going to be away from the coast awhile. I have an apartment in Palisades I'd like you to sit for me while I'm gone.'

'You left making the arrangements a little late.'

'Something came up.'

'You mentioned good money. Good money on an apartment sit makes for small change in any other ball park.'

'Hear me out, Charley.'

Ross Helgstrom had a way of settling into first name terms that left you looking over your shoulder, hoping he was talking to somebody else.

'The proposition stinks, Helgstrom. Nobody breaks into apartments any more, not since the Supreme Court's Forty-Nine ruling on Justifiable Intruder Homicide. Go stock up on AFTDs. Do yourself a favour.'

Even with contacts like Hogie Corcoran it shouldn't have been necessary to remind Helgstrom of the Forty-Nine Supreme Court ruling that intruder homicide was justifiable on any and every occasion, without exception. Overnight, the incident of burglary almost zeroed out as a statistic while the homicide rate — justified or otherwise — went through the roof. For some reason this made a lot of folks happy.

Drunk wives found themselves with a cast iron defence when they blew the old man away after he staggered home at two-thirty a.m. with a gut full of Manhattans, a nose full of coke, and another woman's perfume sweetening his secondhand excuses. Securistores sprang up all over doing gold cred business in Anti-Felon Termination Devices. Booby Lasers put Dobermans out to pasture for good when word got around that a Booby Laser didn't need feeding ten pounds of raw meat every day, and any thieves around who hadn't, or couldn't, read the papers found they left their fingers behind along with the fingerprints when they dipped into the micro-nuked wall safe for the family ice.

'Charley,' Helgstrom said. 'Do yourself a favour. Make yourself some black coffee. Pop some aspirin. Then go check your cred update. I'll call from the airport, okay?'

Helgstrom hung up and I took his advice on the coffee. High Mountain roast. Fresh ground, my regular blend. Then I got on with the kind of things a guy usually does after he's come home too drunk, too pissed with life, to make it out of his clothes and into bed. I took a cold shower, climbed into some fresh dudes, swallowed a pint of OJ straight from the ice-box. Then I brewed some more coffee, dropped the heat with two fingers of Old Crow Bourbon, and swallowed it down in one.

After that, I did like Helgstrom had said, and checked my domestic comp. The accounts window showed a cred-upgrade of five thousand dollars, input eight-forty-five a.m., April 1. Query gave me the additional information that the input was standing order basis, upgrade due at seven day intervals, open ended. It was some salary for an apartment sitter. I parked myself on the sofa, lit up a Heaven's Door, and considered why Ross Helgstrom should be willing to lay that much cred on a gumshoe just to have him go round water his potted plants.

After a while, I gave up thinking about it.

At nine-fifteen, right on schedule, my domestic comp pumped out the morning edition of the *LA Island Post*. For a change, the news wasn't all bad. In the top right hand corner it told me what I already knew, that it was Tuesday, April 1, nine-fifteen a.m.. Further down, the banner headline read: '48-HOUR CEASE-FIRE IN EUROPE!' It was good news for everybody, except maybe, for the multi-national armament corporations, and the front-line body collection squads — the 'body-baggers' stationed along the west slopes of the Rhône-Sâone Valley, Southern France. All over the globe conflict prediction analysts would be breathing a sigh of relief and cancelling the shuttle reservations they'd made for their wives, kids, and mistresses for anywhere south of the equator.

The second big story told me that the Disney Corporation had announced plans to build a replica of London Town the way it was before the opening salvos of the European War of Unification had reduced it to a heap of red hot radioactive rubble. A site due west of Kingsman, Arizona, had been selected, and the intention was to excavate a canal linking up with the Colorado River so that Old Father Thames could keep right on rolling. The waters of the Colorado had been over-subscribed for as long as anybody could remember and, as usual, it was the gold cred Palm Springs golfing fraternity who were blowing up the biggest storm. It took a lot more than fond memories of Frank Sinatra to keep those rolling fairways green. A spokesperson for the Disney Corporation Planning Division was quoted as saying: 'Those guys are going to have to realise... it's not a bunch of dirt farmers they're dealing with here.'

It was ten-fifteen, and I was through to the funnies, when the phone finally rang. I picked up the receiver and said: 'Thanks, but no thanks. Not unless you're prepared to kick back to the top and level with me.'

'I know what you're thinking, Charley,' Hetty said. 'But, you've got it wrong. There's nobody else in the frame.'

'I'm going to need a moment to adjust, here.'

'You've been thinking that all along, right?'

Some days you just can't help but get it wrong every time. It was shaping up into one of those days.

'Hetty...'

'You know I love you, Charley. Don't ever doubt it. It's just...'

'Hetty, I was expecting another call.'

'I just wanted to tell you I was sorry... walking out on you like that last night.'

'Can I get back to you?'

'Hey, Charley, I thought this was supposed to be important to you. To us.'

'That wasn't the way it was last night. Wasn't it you telling me we should keep it uncomplicated, no big deal?'

'Charley?'

'Look, I'll call you back. You're at the station house, right?'

'Do me a big favour, would you, Charley? Just kiss off!'

There didn't seem any point in talking to a dead line so I cradled the receiver. The bell rang again immediately. It was Ross Helgstrom, and my morning for everybody ringing up to apologise.

'Sorry, Charley, I couldn't find a phone at the airport. I'm calling from the shuttle.'

It might have been dumb arrogance or it might have been just plain dumb. 'Helgstrom,' I said, 'would you mind holding the line for just a minute?' I put the receiver down, crossed to the picture-window and pulled the venetians. A laser blast of LA Island sunlight reduced my pupils to pinpricks. I knew what I was going to say, despite that the whole proposition stank.

Blame it on the hang-over.

Blame it on today I was everybody's April Fool.

Blame it on Hetty.

Why the hell not.

I went back to the telephone. 'You still there, Helgstrom?'

'Touchdown in fifteen minutes, Charley. You got to make this quick.'

'You got yourself a deal,' I said.

Helgstrom gave me his address in Palisades and code clearance so his Securistore agent could fix me up AFTD-friendly at the apartment. Another voice joined the conversation. One of the cabin crew hustling him to get back to his seat and belt up.

'Got to go, Charley,' he said. 'These birds don't stack easy.' And hung up.

I mixed cold coffee with cold bourbon and stood at the picture-window staring at the green sky over the tops of the buildings. Then I looked down into the canyon between my apartment block and the one across the way.

Imagined what it would be like to jump.

Chapter Two

'I look at it this way,' Smoky Griscom said, raising a cold can of Michelob — his fourth in the past hour — to his lips. 'There's but four categories. Those who won't, those who can't, those who can, and those who have to.'

'Yeah,' I said, 'and those who have to always figure they're on the list with those who can.'

'I handle my booze.'

'How do you know that, Smoky? I never seen you without you got a drink in your hand.'

Smoky chuckled.

From deep down in his throat.

Then he spat out over the gunwale. The gob of phlegm sat there in the ocean like an aborted Portuguese man o'war.

It was four-thirty p.m., we were aboard Smoky's cruiser, the *Rosita Recherché*, and it was a long afternoon away from my conversation over the telephone with Ross Helgstrom, Hetty's attempt at conciliation, and my hard cold stare into the canyon of empty air beneath my apartment block.

First time I ever met Smoky Griscom, seven years back, I'd been thinking about jumping then, too. Leaning over the guard rail on the Santa Monica Pier, counting the waves, hoping the rail might snap.

Just one more decision I could avoid making for myself.

'You ever been shark fishing?' Smoky had said, parking himself alongside me at the rail, smiling, like he always does when there's not a lot to be smiling about. Sharp blue eyes freeze-framed between avarice and mischief. Tall sinewy build taking in the slack from the offshore breeze. A five and ten store yachting hat perched on the back of his head, the grey stubble of his crew-cut holding it there, like velcro.

'I got no beef with sharks,' I said.

'Me, neither, son,' Smoky replied. 'That's why I make it a point never hooking into one. These waters, a great white can make twenty feet, weigh in at seven thousand pounds. Tow you clear across to Hawaii, one of those bastards.'

Smoky laughed. It was infectious. After we were through laughing, I said, 'Sure, I'll go shark fishing with you. Why the hell not?'

Since then we had gotten into the habit.

With some folks it was meditation.

Others, another man's wife.

For me, it was shark fishing with Smoky Griscom.

The *Rosita Recherché*– or, *Rosita* 'Rechurch', which was how Smoky said it — was a 30-foot, six-berth, cabin cruiser. Rigged at the stern with comp-controlled robo-tackle, it could drag six hundred yards of thirty-six thread through any swell the Pacific Ocean could work up between the coast of California and that off-shore island of cinder waste the cartographers used to call Japan. Smoky had bought the *Rosita* cheap from an old guy he met in the Quarter Deck, a berth-holders-only joint across from the jetty in Marina Del Rey. They shook hands on the deal over a quart of bonded Jack Daniels and Smoky had taken the *Rosita* out that same night. The bar-keep at the Quarter Deck, who had been asked to witness the transaction, said Smoky always had been the kind of guy who liked to learn port from starboard the hard way. Knowing Smoky, like I do now, I figured he was just trying to distance himself from the old man's sad stories and repossessed dreams. Most folks who consider themselves sensitive never get to see beyond their own problems. With Smoky, it was the other way around. Smoky laughed a lot, but those tears in his eyes were for real.

'You ready for another?' Without waiting for a reply, Smoky pulled a fresh six-pack from the ice-box stowed against the gunwale, peeled two cans, and handed one to me.

I flicked the tab into an empty bait-bucket.

The *Rosita* was drifting slowly south, pulled by the cool waters of the Herga Current, trailing a hundred feet of line with a tuna bait. We got a strike, Smoky would run with it a while, then free the line. To the east, the black line of derelict off-shore oil rigs, stretching from horizon to horizon, cut off our view of the mainland. This time in the afternoon, with the haze building up over the water and heat refraction playing tricks with your eyes, you could almost imagine LA Island City was still a sleepy adobe mission, stuck there between the desert and the sea. Imagine how it was way back when, before the Conquistadors retreated south, and the European settlers found a trail through the Rocky Mountains to build an empire based on oil, talking-pictures, and a life-style where the dream and the reality came so close, nobody could tell the difference anymore.

Smoky, seeing I was through talking awhile, went below to fix us some pastrami on rye.

There were still plenty of pleasure craft out on the water and I didn't pay any particular attention to the powder-blue power boat that nosed out through one of the navigation channels between the oil rigs until it set a course that would head-reach our southerly drift. The power boat was moving fast, bows well clear of the water.

I stuck my head down the hatch.

'You expecting company, Smoky? Two guys in a powder-blue Eventrude?'

Smoky shook his head.

I climbed up the companionway to the bridge, grabbed Smoky's binoculars and focused on the power boat. The guy not pumping gas was strapped into a fishing rig at the stern. He had a rifle raised to his shoulder fitted with a telescopic sight. We stared at each other, close-focus through our separate lenses, as he stopped breathing and squeezed. The first solid-state whined across the quarter deck. The second shell punched a hole above the water-line on the port side, then punched a larger hole exiting to starboard.

Smoky quit slicing pastrami and poked his head up the companionway.

'What the hell was that!?'

A third shell shattered the for'ard cabin window, ricocheted around some, then blew a hole in the cabin roof.

'Stay down, Smoky,' I yelled. 'Keep below the water-line.'

I slid down from the bridge and pushed Smoky back into the galley. The power boat was making a ninety degree turn, its stern biting deep into the water, throwing up a white cascade of ocean which momentarily obscured the craft, before it reappeared circling the *Rosita Recherché*.

'Is there a piece on board?'

'Charley, who needs a shooter on a fishing trip?'

I could have come up with a reply just as dumb but, right now, wise-cracks were out of season. There was a bump as the Eventrude came alongside and a voice, over the gunwale, said: 'You guys want to throw us a line?'

I went ahead of Smoky up onto the quarterdeck. Smoky threw a line to the guy at the wheel, who secured it, then cut the engine. The punk strapped into the fishing rig was cradling the rifle like it was his newborn baby brother. He had stone-blue eyes, an incipient moustache, and crooked teeth. The rifle was a Winchester 44 solid state. It packed a soft-nosed self-propellant slug, effective over five miles, with infra-red comp-vector auto-adjust sights.

When the kid smiled, it was all trick and no treat.

The other guy was older, well-dressed in an expensive cut black silicon suit, shooting white cuffs, and sporting expensive gold links. He held up a hand, 'Help me up here, will ya,' he said, then, over his shoulder to the kid: 'This is the one to watch, you hear that, Pauli?'

'Loud and clear, Spook,' the kid said.

Spook had got it exactly right. As he got his foot on the gunwale, I pulled him forward into the line of fire and gut punched him has hard as I could make it. Spook grunted and doubled up on the deck reaching for his inside pocket. I dumped a bucket of tuna meat bait over the side at Pauli, hearing the bucket connect, then brought my foot down on Spook's wrist as the Colt Cremator came clear.

'You want I should break your wrist?'

Spook released his grip on the gun.

'Fuckhead!'

I gathered up the Colt Cremator and turned it, two-fisted down towards Pauli in the Eventrude. The Winchester was laying in front of him, out of reach on the deck of the power boat. Pauli was struggling to release the harness that strapped him to the fishing rig. I should have done him a favour right then and blown him away. His face and vest were a mess of tuna meat. More tuna meat was floating in the water beyond the power boat, spreading circles of blood. The water stirred and a grey dorsal broke surface. Spook was on his feet by now. He'd seen the shark, too.

'Jes–us!'

The shark reared out of the water, mouth wide, eyes rolled back in its head, as it hit the power boat, smashing the hull in two, midship. Pauli had released the harness. As the shark struck, he toppled over backwards into the water, too frightened to even scream. The bow section of the Eventrude, housing the weight of the engine, sank immediately. The stern section, with the fishing rig, rolled away from the *Rosita* slowly, sank slowly. As the *Rosita* keeled over, Smoky Griscom severed the line that joined the two craft, leaving the stricken stern of the Eventrude to tango down through the deep in pursuit of hot metal and gasoline spillage.

Pauli broke surface, spat water, then was gone.

'Jesus!' Spook said, again.

I cold-cocked him with the Cremator before he could come out of shock.

Flanagan's, across the jetty from where Smoky Griscom rented a permanent berth for the *Rosita* alongside Marquesa Way, Marina Del Rey, was one of those low-life bars turned respectable, with framed photographs of the owner all over the walls. The photographs told you nothing except, maybe, everybody has to get old, sometime. Flanagan was of Irish-black descent, a retired middle-weight boxer who used to have all the serious money running behind him until The Syndicate persuaded him to take a dive to stay alive, back in Forty-Two. Since then, it had been all downhill. The photographs showed a young guy in zippy silk pants throwing a right hook at everything the future had to offer. The guy behind the bar had a nose spread like a kangaroo rat caught in the headlights on Route Three into Palm Springs, a hair-line at low tide, and a row of crevasses across his brow that told you more about his history than a tree surgeon could divine from counting the rings on the decapitated stump of a giant redwood. You didn't believe the lines, all you had to do was look into Flanagan's eyes.

'Use the telephone?' I asked.

'Long distance or local?'

'It's so local, maybe I should just go back out on the sidewalk and shout.'

'Suit yourself, bud. Either way, it don't bother me none.' Flanagan pushed the phone across the counter.

'While I'm on this, how about you build me a Jack Daniels, straight up. Tall one.'

'I don't need no favours, mister.'

'Sure,' I said, 'build the drink, will you?'

I punched in the digits for the Santa Monica Precinct House. Halloran, the desk sergeant caught the call and, when I asked for Malloy, patched me straight through.

'Squad room, Malloy speaking,' Patrick said.

I could see him at his desk, over by the steel shuttered window, on the second floor, an unlit filter straight stuck between the blades of his teeth, a heap of hard copy comp printouts building a wall between himself and a regular six hour shift, a plastic beaker of coffee, perched at his elbow, that wasn't going to taste any better now it was cold.

'Two gunsels, Spook and Pauli — you got anything on them?'

'Charley.'

'In one, Patrick.'

'So, small talk makes you vomit. I don't mind, Charley. All that long time no see, how's the wife, how's the kid's — who needs it, right?'

'So how's Marlene... how's Josh and Patch?'

'Don't make me laugh, Charley. These two goons — what else you got?'

'That's it, Patrick.'

'Central Comp is just like flesh and blood, Charley. The more you give, the more you get.'

'People keep telling me that and I would like to believe them.'

'Registered names, date and place of birth, ID tags, known associates, you with me on this?'

'Patrick, I know all that…'

'But you don't Charley.'

'That's why the call, Patrick.'

Malloy cradled the phone and punched keys. 'Nothing, Charley,' he said, after a moment.

'Nothing?'

'What you want, I should make it up?'

'Patrick,' I said, 'you're a good cop, but being a good cop don't take imagination.'

Malloy sighed.

'You mind telling me what this is about, Charley?'

The Jack Daniels was on the bar in front of me, tall, straight up, just like I'd order. I let it sit there while I told Malloy about my afternoon fishing trip with Smoky Griscom.

'Poor bastard.'

That was Pauli.

And the shark.

'All his life, Patrick,' I said.

Flanagan moved closer. He was all ears, despite they were cauliflowered against the side of his head.

'The gunsel, Spook — where is he now?'

'Aboard the *Rosita* with Smoky. He's got a cracked head, Smoky's got a gun. I don't see a problem.'

'All my life, people been telling me that. Your pal, Griscom?'

'You heard of the Griscom Institute of Primordial Correctness?'

'That Griscom!'

'One in the same.'

The Griscom Institute of Primordial Correctness had centres all over the country where, for a fat fee, old ladies, bored with wintering on the Keys, and tired executives looking to put some macho back into their lives, enrolled on a two week seminar. The course was designed to take them back to basics, reteach them the comfort of open fires and fresh running water, the joy of ripping raw meat with their bare hands, the aphrodisiac qualities of natural body odour.

It was a doozy of an idea, and Smoky Griscom went mega-cred in twelve short months.

Five years back, the FBI had investigated the Institute and later introduced an amended version of the course into their agent indoctrination curriculum at Camp David, Maryland. Smoky billed the Treasury Department for a fat fee, then sued when they refused to pay up. He dropped the litigation after a posse of Internal Revenue snoops descended on his suite of offices on Divisidero. Smoky wasn't that much of a caveman that he couldn't make the connection.

'So, who were they coming at, Charley,' Malloy asked. 'You or Griscom?'

'Why don't you get down here, Patrick, ask the guy yourself.'

'My priorities don't allow for that. Here on LA Island we get a homicide report every thirty-two seconds, day and night. All you got is a boat full of holes and a shark attack, presumed fatality. Why don't you call the Sheriff's Office?'

Flanagan had grown tired of listening to one end of a conversation and looked about ready to throw his famous right hook. The bar was filling up with after work drinkers. He didn't like me confusing his bar with my office.

'Tell you what I'll do, Patrick,' I said. 'I'll go back on over to the *Rosita*, zap the gunsel one more time, and dump him in the harbour. How does that grab you?'

Malloy sighed. 'Stay put, Charley,' he said.

I cradled the phone, drank the bourbon, and headed for the door.

'Only the phone call comes free, mister,' Flanagan called after me.

'On Smoky's tab, will you?'

Outside, dusk had fallen with the speed it always does in LA Island City. The navigation lights and anti-collision sensors on the boats still cruising the main concourse of the marina where like somebody had decorated the harbour for Thanksgiving. Overhead, a local 897 was carving a pink vapour trail through a purple sky. Over on Lincoln, I could hear the homebound commuter traffic building to a standstill. Sometimes, it seemed crazy to think there were people out there holding down a steady job.

My Plymouth Pulsar was parked alongside Smoky's Rolls Royce Expatriate at the jetty. Smoky's Rolls had a leopard-skin rag-top and white-walled tyres. My Pulsar looked like a trash can left out by the Roller for overnight collection. I climbed in and gunned the motor, straight eight, firing on seven. As I hit Admiralty Way and hung a left towards Lincoln, the auto-comp cut in with a burst of static. 'Seat Belt...Seat Belt...Seat Belt...' it said.

I reached under my seat, found the plastic wedge I kept stowed there, and jammed it into the clip of the safety harness.

Over the silence, I said: 'Dumb fuckin' machine.'

Chapter Three

Eddy 'The Peep' Lagunda, the only son of a high cred grape farmer from the San Joaquin Valley, had been two years old when, in Fifty-Three, the Californian State Commission on Educational Reform had bulldozed the groves of academe and implemented the new DNI (Direct Neural Implantation) technology which had already proved so successful on the East Coast. The realty speculators made a killing and, by the time Eddy reached college age, the UCLAI campus had become one more jungle of gold cred condominiums, leisure complexes, and total environment shopping malls.

It was a tough break for Eddy. With his good looks, his ginger-blond hair curled tight as a gym mat to his skull, he was designer-cast for the part — A-Team quarter-back, frat house president, plucking sport scholarships out of the system as effortlessly and mechanically as his old man plucked grapes from the vine. The envy of all those poor creeps left behind in the locker room with a complexion problem and no date for the Graduation Ball; those same poor creeps who featured on the FBI comp analysis profiles as statistically most likely to burn a president, waste a rock star, or take out ten lanes of peak hour San Diego Freeway traffic with a laser-charged Armstrong Enfilader.

Sure, it was a tough break for Eddy. But, then, Eddy had no way of knowing what he had missed and, who knows, maybe Eddy himself would have ended up featuring on those FBI profiles. It was always the campus stars who got drop-kicked the hardest by the real world outside once the cheer leaders quit dancing on the touch-line.

I'd arranged to meet Eddy at Sweets Bar, on Sunset, at seven-fifteen. It was seven-forty-five when I pulled into the forecourt and handed the keys to a kid wearing retractable rollers, a velvet-blue track suit, and a baseball cap which read: 'SWEET ON YOU'.

'Take care of the paintwork, kid,' I said. 'This automobile bites back.'

The kid moved a wad of gum from one jaw bone to the other, gave the Pulsar a once-over, then concertinaed his long body into the driver's seat.

'Mister, if I had a dollar for every promise.'

He slammed the car door and took off towards a vacant space, throwing up gravel like it was popcorn on a red hot stove.

At reception, a blonde wearing black tights, black suspenders, and a vacant expression checked out my plastic. She didn't seem to be enjoying her job any better than the kid out front parking cars. The comp monitor came up three cherries in a row and she handed me back my card with a smile that had seen a lot of mirror. A smile that, one sweet day, might lead to a screen-test, the casting couch, and upward mobility into the movie industry.

With kids, the dreams and the nightmares sometimes got all mixed up.

I pushed through the revolving door into the bar and Eddy waved to me from a table across the room. He was sitting with a blonde he introduced as Rita. Sweets Bar was a good place for blondes. I said hello to Rita and sat down while Eddy ordered the drinks.

Eddy 'The Peep' Lagunda was a small time private investigator, with an office in Pasadena, who made big money supplying glossy prints that could build the alimony and give the prosecution an easy time. When that line of work came my way I would pass it on to Eddy. He reciprocated with anything that looked like he might get his ass burnt off on the wrong end of a Colt Cremator.

That was why Eddy always paid for the drinks.

'Sorry, I kept you waiting, Eddy,' I said.

Eddy Lagunda spread his hands. He had a ring on every finger and cuticles cut clean as a baby. 'Hey, what are friends for,' Eddy said.

'You tell me, Eddy,' I said. 'I've spent a lifetime trying to figure it out.'

Eddy laughed.

It wasn't infectious.

Rita looked at me like I'd just told her she was catching the tab for the evening's entertainment.

After the drinks arrived, I filled Eddy in on what I had. It wasn't much, but it was what kept Eddy in white silicon suits and blondes who didn't go a bundle on my line in jokes. A guy called Jake Lomax had been on to me to supply the goods on his wife, Petra. They had been married for twelve years. Happily, according to Lomax. Six months back, Petra had suddenly taken it into her head that there might be more to life than throwing coronaries over the kids and fooling around with the function console on the domestic comp. Her first move had been into the guest room, where she sat up all night reading all kinds of weirdo books. Her second was to enrol in the Westward Chapter of the Secular Order of Creative Celibacy, which met every Wednesday night in the upstairs function room of Lipo-Sucks Sisters Only Work-Out Parlour, on Benvita. Her line to Lomax was that she figured it was time she was channelling her energies into something a little more rewarding than keeping Jake warm in the sack every Saturday night after he staggered home from an evening shooting pool with the boys.

'Can you blame the lady,' Rita said, shaking around the permacubes in her glass before killing the scotch with one shot.

'Nobody's blaming anybody,' I said.

'The point being,' Eddy said, 'it will be Jake Lomax catching the tab, not his old lady.'

Eddy 'The Peep' Lagunda liked his limousines fast and silent. He liked his women the same way — which meant he didn't expect them to interrupt when he was discussing business. Maybe Rita hadn't been around long enough to understand the ground rules. Or maybe she had, and was all washed up with bothering to keep Eddy happy.

'The point being, Eddy,' I said, 'Jake Lomax doesn't buy his wife's story. He figures she's holding out on him because there's another guy in the frame. He wants to know what she gets up to every Wednesday night when she's supposed to be spacing out on group therapy and preparing her body for the muse to take her.'

Eddy spread his hands, again.

'No problem,' he said. 'Outside of the muse, anybody takes that dame, I'm gonna know about it.'

'Eddy,' I said, 'with mitts like that you'd have made a great catcher.'

I bored Eddy with the details, thanked him for the drink, and tried to make it past the blonde in reception without she gave me another of her sweet and low smiles.

Fat chance.

'Get home safe, you hear, now,' she said.

'I'll do that,' I said. 'Just so long as the kid in the forecourt leaves me some tread.'

Traffic was light. I made it to Ross Helgstrom's apartment block across from the beach on Montana, Palisades, in fifteen minutes, no change down. As I curbed the Pulsar, the auto-comp gave me a run-down on mean local temperature, humidity, and toxic count. I should have listened. A warm blanket of heat wrapped itself around my shoulders as I hit the sidewalk, leaving me tired, slack-limbed, and pissed with having to hustle for a living. High overhead an intercontinental shuttle bounced into the hard shoulder of the ionosphere, a lone shooting star above a city that denied the existence of life elsewhere. Over the Pacific, a full moon just hung there, pointing a finger of light across the water and between the palms that divided Palisades Park and the coastal highway.

There was a couple walking the dog.

An old guy with a brown bag and a quart bottle.

A kid, on blades, heading home for supper.

But, it was me the moon was watching.

Ross Helgstrom's apartment block overlooked the park and the ocean. There was a stretch of lawn, and a security guard who had lost his faith in human nature the first day he opened his pay-packet. I showed him my ID and took the elevator up to the top floor. There were two doors in a large hall, and a floor generating anti-grav that left you feeling like Jesus Christ walking on the water. Helgstrom's apartment was 221. I showed plastic to the surveillance monitor, listened while the anti-felon bolts disengaged, then pushed through the door and found a light switch.

At Grauman's Chinese Theatre, when the house lights went up, it meant the show was over. In Ross Helgstrom's apartment it worked the other way around. There was a mezzanine lounge and a recessed, white tiled, dining area, the furniture high-tech and functional. The venetians were drawn on a wall to wall picture window and the moon was still hanging over the ocean. Only now, it wasn't me it was looking at. The dead woman staining Helgstrom's carpet lay on her stomach, her arms folded, cradling her head, one leg drawn up, as if she had fallen asleep. There were two ugly entry wounds between her shoulder blades, close spaced, grouped to take out her heart through the front of her chest. When the Police Department ME finally showed up he was going to reach the same conclusion as me. Nobody falls that way when they've been kicked in the back by a couple of solid state slugs from a heavy duty canon. It didn't take a florist to appreciate that somebody had been rearranging the flowers.

The woman had been in her early thirties, good looking, with red hair, rough cut, rotogene style. She was wearing electric-blue jeans and what was left of a matching top. On her right hand, she had three rings, one of them a band of gold.

I knelt down and placed two fingers against her throat, along the line of the carotid artery, beneath her left ear.

She was cold.

Inanimate.

I drew my hand away, quickly.

'It's a shock every time, right?'

I stood up and turned around.

The woman that went with the voice came out of the kitchen with a drink in her hand. She was tall, sleepy eyed, bleached hair shaved close behind the ears, long on top, supported by pearl anti-grav sequins. She moved like a dancer, slim and athletic, in a grey jump suit, and brown leather *huaraches* like the pavement musicians wear along Ocean Front Walk on a Sunday afternoon.

'Some things, you just never get used to,' I said.

'Some things, who needs to get used to?'

She sat down on the sofa, curling her long legs beneath her.

'You're not a cop.'

It wasn't a question, but I answered anyway.

'No, I'm not a cop. Would it make any difference?'

She shrugged.

'I'm no priest, either, lady,' I said. 'But, if it's a confessional you're looking for, go right ahead.'

'You think I killed her?'

'I like to keep an open mind.'

'Watch out. Your kind is an endangered species.'

'Don't lose sleep on my account.'

'Sounds like that might be fun.'

I left the innuendo hanging there, like a skeet about to get shattered. She counted the ice-cubes in her drink, then took a sip.

'Isn't this about the time we should be introducing ourselves?'

'Be my guest.'

'Travesty Coombe-Lately,' she said, holding out a hand. 'But, spare me the jokes. I've heard them all before.'

Her hand was one more thing I left hanging there.

'I never crack jokes when somebody is waving a double-barrel in my face.'

'Private dick.'

That wasn't a question, either.

'Travesty, you want to tell me what's going on?'

She smiled.

'I rang a guy I know in San Francisco. He told me nothing was happening right now in San Francisco. I came here, instead.'

'And you believed this guy?'

'You got to believe somebody, sometime.'

'Sometime, maybe,' I said.

I found the telephone on a bookcase, resting between a stack of blue movies and a collection of jazz magazines.

'You calling the cops?'

'What do you think?'

The phone was just what you would expect to find in a bachelor apartment. A moulded plastic, hand-painted Mickey Mouse. I untangled Mickey's right arm and prodded my finger into his chest to dial the Santa Monica Precinct House. Halloran was still on duty. He asked me to hold the line.

Travesty Coombe-Lately was over at the wet bar fixing herself another drink. I watched her scoop ice, top up with white rum, lime, and grated nutmeg.

Then Malloy was on the line.

'Charley, you're playing games with me.'

'No games, Patrick,' I said. 'Right now, I'm at 221 Palisades in the company of a homicide victim and a murder one suspect.'

Malloy betrayed no surprise.

'Your busy day, Charley.'

Detective First Grade Patrick Malloy, despite his name, was from a long line of native American Apache stock. His old man had changed the family name, and christened his first-born son, Patrick, as a gesture to his hunting buddy, Mayor Timothy Patrick Malloy, who had pulled civic strings to grant him a ski resort franchise up on Lake Arrowhead. It wasn't in Patrick Malloy's nature to betray surprise.

Or any other emotion.

'So, how come you didn't stick around?'

'I figured it didn't need both of us wasting our time on one cheap gunsel in a state of shock.'

'Well, you figured wrong, Charley. The cheap gunsel got the drop on your pal, Smoky, and was long gone by the time I arrived.'

'Smoky hurt?'

'Only, his pride.'

'You count the holes in the *Rosita*?'

'Sure, I counted the holes, but nobody has to bury a boat.'

'Patrick, I've got two good looking women here with me, right now, and somebody, sure as hell, got to bury one of them.'

'This time, stay put, will you, Charley?'

'That's a promise.'

I replaced Mickey Mouse's right arm on his right shoulder and turned round to see Travesty Coombe-Lately pirouetting towards me across the carpet. I'd seen it all before in the late night Kung Fu movies. Her right leg swung in a wide arc.

Then a foot connected with the side of my head.

When I came round it was just me and the woman on the floor. She still couldn't move.

I could.

But, it wasn't easy.

In Helgstrom's bathroom, I washed my face under the cold tap and stood looking into the mirror, memorising the features that stared back at me, so that next time I ran into a mug I would be able to recognise him.

Then I left the apartment.

Chapter Four

Hetty O'Hara let herself into my Studio View apartment at one-thirty a.m. and found me exchanging sweet nothings with a quart of Old Crow Bourbon that I'd invited home with me for company. The bottle was still three quarters full, but, already, I had a gut reaction the relationship was going someplace.

'You don't need that, Charley,' Hetty said.

She unhitched her shoulder bag and let it fall to the floor. Apart from the usual mess of paraphernalia every woman feels obliged to haul around with her, Hetty's shoulder bag contained a Police Department regulation issue Armstrong Variable and a Colt Cremator. The Colt Cremator was an optional extra. It was also the reason why her shoulder bag hit the floor with the kind of impact a berserko jumper would make, sky-diving from the twenty-fourth storey roof top plaza, at Downtown City Hall.

'What do you know, Hetty?' I said.

'I don't want to fight, okay?'

She knelt beside me on the lounger and laid her head on my lap. I pulled the clip from her hair, allowing it to tumble free, combed her hair with my fingers. We stayed like that awhile, then I put down my drink and she crawled onto my lap. The first kiss was friendly. The second more than that.

'So, what's the big attraction, Hetty?'

'Self-doubt, Charley? Goes with the juice.'

'No, really?'

'Really? I told you, you'd go fuck it up. Maybe, that's what's the big attraction.'

She kissed me, again.

'I like the way you do that,' I said

'Why didn't you call me back, Charley?'

The spell wasn't broken, but, there was a hair-line crack I hadn't noticed before.

'No recriminations, no regrets. Isn't that what you said last night?'

'I didn't want this to happen... you know that, don't you?'

'Why fight it?'

The hair-line crack was gone.

All in my imagination.

'Let's go to bed, Charley,' Hetty said.

Desk security rang a half hour later: 'I got two cops down here to see you. You want I should send them up?'

'Do you have a choice?' I said.

'Charley?'

Hetty's voice from the bed.

'It will keep.'

'Not for ever, Charley.'

I found my dressing-gown and had the door to my apartment open before Malloy could flat-foot the dead-lock. The guy with him was new to me. Dressed like a coat hanger. Everything brand new and hanging from his shoulders like there was nothing underneath but hot air. Plaid check jacket, grey slacks with razor sharp creases. Pale, expressionless face, and blond hair that hung limp to his shoulders.

'Who's your new friend, Patrick?' I said.

'I was starting to think you were a figment of my imagination, Charley.'

'You didn't answer my question.'

'Theo Lipztic, Detective Second Grade, on loan from the New York Police Department. Here to find out how we do it on the West Coast.'

'Lipstick? What kind of name is "Lipstick"?'

Theo's idea of a smile was to expose his teeth. They were even enough, but yellow, like his hair.

'Polish — got more z's in it than a fuckhead like you could handle. Back on the 82nd, they call me "Collar".'

'Collar?'

'*Lipstick On Your Collar*, old Connie Francis song, get it?'

'That why they sent you out west, Theo — develop your sense of humour?'

'Back East, you think I'd put up with this shit?'

'There's a shuttle lifts off every hour, on the hour,' I said. 'I'd hate for you to feel repressed.'

Malloy stood there, his bulk filling most of the door, saying nothing, as if the exchange was a necessary formality that had to be got through and then forgotten.

'You guys coming in, or what?'

'Get dressed, Charley.'

'Come on, Patrick, you know what time it is?'

'Sure, I know what time it is.'

'And this can't wait till the morning?'

'You've been giving me the run around all day, Charley.'

'How about I cuff the bastard,' Theo Lipztic said.

He was already reaching for his belt clip.

'Butt out, Theo!' Malloy said.

In the State of California, despite on-line link-up with Federal Central Comp, the Police Department still had nowhere to run from a mountain of paperwork. Everything had to be strictly hard copy print out, in triplicate, retained and filed. Bureaucracy is a many headed Hydra, and every head had a desk down at City Hall and a fat pay cheque to protect.

To Detective First Grade Patrick Malloy, 'user friendly' was a dope-head with a clean needle.

'Daisy Creek,' Malloy said. 'Name mean anything to you?'

'The dead woman?'

'We're asking the questions, Case.'

That was Theo Lipztic.

'How about you send this guy out for some coffee and doughnuts?'

Malloy balled up the print-out he had been reading and tossed it towards the disposal alongside his desk.

It missed.

'Professional dancer. Worked the diner-dance circuits, Palm Springs, Tijuana, Neuvo Las Vegas. Married to a keyboard player, Otis Webster Creek, with an address in Pensacola, Alabama.'

'Any connection with Helgstrom?'

'Yeah,' Malloy said. 'She was his sister.'

Across the squad room a fax began clattering at an empty desk. The fug of stale tobacco hung in the air like smoke over a bomb crater.

'You trace Helgstrom?'

'Shuttle to New York, Kennedy. Rented a Budget car at the airport. No stop-offs for gas or food, no hotel reservations. Must have stayed local, spent the night with friends.' Malloy shrugged. 'Next time he uses plastic, we'll find him.'

'What about the other woman?'

'No record. According to Federal Central Comp, she doesn't exist.'

'Yeah,' I said. 'So, I got drop kicked by an apparition.'

'Could be it was a classified apparition, Charley?'

'What are you saying?'

'You work it out.'

'Federal involvement?'

'Who would you sooner be dealing with, Charley, me or the Feds?'

'That one's too easy.'

'Okay, try this one: what were you really doing in Helgstrom's apartment?'

'I already told you.'

Malloy stared at me like I'd just asked him to sign one more treaty allowing the Union Pacific Railroad to carve up his ancestral prairies. 'We checked your cred status, Charley. Yesterday morning Ross Helgstrom paid five thousand dollars into your account.'

'To sit his apartment.'

'Suppose, I don't buy that?'

'Why not? I did.'

Theo Lipztic had been silent all this time. Now, he leant his palms on Malloy's desk.

'This goes nowhere,' he said.

Malloy looked up at him.

'Back east you got a different way of doing things, am I right?'

'You want I should demonstrate?'

I smiled at Theo.

'Maybe, I got it wrong. I thought your role here was as an observer?'

'So far, fuck-head, I don't see much I can take home with me.'

'Theo,' Malloy said, 'why don't you go get yourself that coffee — and bring me one back with you?'

'Mine's two sugars, no cream,' I said.

'Screw you!'

'Theo?'

That was Malloy.

'Screw the both of you!'

After he was gone, Malloy said, 'What's going on, Charley?'

'Patrick, it's been one hell of a day.'

'You know I could hold you on suspicion of withholding information?'

'But, you wouldn't want to give Theo the pleasure.'

'You're right, Charley, I wouldn't.'

Downstairs in the muster-room, Sergeant Halloran was checking tomorrow's form behind the brass rail of the rostrum. Behind him were three rows of empty desks. During the day shift those desks were occupied by comp liaison clerks. On the far wall a clock with walnut finish and roman numerals told me it was three-forty-five a.m. Halloran had rescued that clock from the rubble of the Big One of Ninety-Seven and lovingly restored it. It was in the guide books as the oldest working clock in LA Island City. On one of a row of seats over by the door sat a tall, angular woman with high Spanish cheek-bones. She didn't look like a hooker or a crime casualty. Maybe, she was waiting for the bail bondsman to come down, release her old man, or son, out onto the street where he could do some more damage.

'How goes it, Halloran,' I said.

'Quiet for a Tuesday night, Charley,' Halloran said. 'But, then, Tuesday always was a quiet night.'

It was Halloran's way of reminding me he was Irish.

The woman got up from her seat and came over. She held out her hand. 'Estelle Scriven,' she said. 'The desk sergeant, here, told me you might be able to help me, if I waited.'

Halloran gave me an exaggerated wink.

'If it's a lift you want, I'm headed for Century City. I'm parked in the basement pound.'

'Can we talk in your car?'
'Sure, if you don't mind interruptions from the auto-comp.'
We found the Pulsar in the basement. Estelle Scriven curled up into the passenger seat beside me, and I gunned the motor up the ramp and out onto Santa Monica Boulevard. The auto-comp went through a list of statistical probabilities relating to what time in the morning it was and suggested reselection to auto-drive.
'See what I mean,' I said to Estelle Scriven.
A black and white was parked out front of the precinct house and two uniformed cops were hustling a kid up the steps. One of the cops had the kid's arm twisted up behind his back like he was demonstrating there was no place you couldn't scratch if you set your mind to it. The cruiser's hazard lights were flashing, bouncing white light off the darkened storefront windows across the street. Big Joe's Doughnut and Grill was still open, but the joint was empty.
I made five sets of green in a row before the auto-comp gave up lecturing me on retarded metabolism and reactive capability. There were three more greens ahead, followed by a red. I shifted into top and pumped gas as the single red fell in line with the others.
'You're a private detective, right?' Estelle Scriven said.
'I prefer confidential consultant. It has more style.'
'Either way, you come highly recommended.'
'By Halloran? Maybe, he was just trying to get you off his back. What the hell were you doing there at this Godforsaken hour anyway?'
'Waiting to find a cop interested in finding my husband.'
'You married?'
'That's the way it goes when you have a husband. You disappointed?'
Estelle Scriven was all Hispanic. Raven black hair, olive complexion, but with rogue baby blue eyes that wouldn't have to shed any tears to let you know it was feeding time.
I ignored her question.
'You know the cops won't file a Missing Persons until forty-eight hours has elapsed. When did you last have contact with your husband?'
'It's been eight months, Charley. And all I've been getting is the run around, coast to coast.'

'How come?'

'It's a long story.'

'And it's been a long day. Maybe, you can bore me with it some other time.'

I caught my first red on the junction with Westward.

'Where do you want dropping, Estelle,' I said.

Chapter Five

Estelle Scriven's place was in Glendale, out past where the Santa Monica Boulevard finally ran out of street numbers to become Hyperion, a ranch-house style bungalow with a steeply inclined front lawn, dotted with acacia shrub, on a terraced suburban development built under the shadow of Eagle Rock where every crescent, terrace and drive looked so alike you could get lost just walking the dog round the block to the local hyper-mart.

I pulled over where Estelle told me and left the engine running. Back down in the basin, I could see the lights of the long distance haulage, burning rubber along Ventura, between LA Island City and The Valley. Beyond that, the dark, no-go area which was Griffith Park.

We were parked on a one in five.

'Quiet neighbourhood.'

'I'm house-sitting for some friends.'

'They leave you spiked boots, along with the latch key?'

Estelle smiled. 'It's not so bad, Charley.'

'Call me tomorrow?'

'You don't want a nightcap?'

'It's a long drive.'

'You could always...'

'Call me tomorrow, Estelle.'

It was light by the time I got back to my apartment and the birds would have been singing, only there were no birds left to sing in LA Island City. Hetty was asleep. I poured myself an Old Crow from the bottle I had ditched earlier, took a hot shower, then climbed into bed beside her. I woke up at ten-forty-five. Hetty was gone. In the indentation left by her head on the pillow was a note. It said: 'It's not easy, loving you, Charley. Catch you later.'

I thought about that note, awhile.

Overall, it left me feeling good. In the kitchen, the OJ container was empty and the lid was off the High Mountain Roast. A dirty cup sat on the draining board, a filter straight stubbed out in the saucer beside it. The domestic comp screen was querying: *'Further Instruction?'*

I flamed a Heaven's Door, went through to the lounge and opened the venetians. Outside was all grey-green smog.

The sun was up there, somewhere, consolidating its supply lines, waiting to scorch the streets in a new offensive. It was easy to forget LA Island was sat in a desert. Easy to forget that, three hundred years back, when the Franciscan monks hauled their pack mules up El Camino Riale from what is now The People's Democratic Republic of Mexico, all they found, when they reached Our Lady Queen of Angels, was dry mesquite, circling condors and water holes running black with oil. I turned away from the window. The domestic comp was still waiting on further instructions, so I punched in an upgrade on air-conditioning. Then I cleared up Hetty's mess in the kitchen and brewed some coffee. When the telephone rang, I had the feeling it would be bad news. It was Hogie Corcoran.

'Charley, we need to talk.'

'So, go ahead.'

'Can we meet, someplace?'

'Hogie, it sounds like you got a problem. You want to tell me about it?'

'You know Rosco's? All day breakfast joint, off the Venice Front?'

'Sure, I know Rosco's. Best link sausage in town, and all the coffee you can drink for three dollars fifty, just so long as you don't mind the company you keep.'

'Can you meet me there in a half hour?'

'That depends, Hogie.'

Hogie had to think about that.

After he was through thinking, he said: 'Did a guy called Ross Helgstrom ever get in touch with you?'

'Sure, he did. I owe you a big favour, Hogie, you putting that guy on to me.'
'Hey, what was I to know?'
'Maybe, less than you know now?'
'Charley...'
'Tell me about Helgstrom, Hogie.'
'Like what, Charley?'
'Like how you got to be like that with a guy can afford an apartment overlooking the ocean on Palisades?'
'It wasn't like that, Charley.'
'So, what was it like?'
'He put work my way.'
'What kind of work?'
'Like, a guy over in Culver owes him two big ones, I go over and collect.'
'How did you meet up with him?'
'He used to drop by the bar of an evening. We got talking. You know how it goes. I'm telling you exactly the same as I told the two guys came round this morning asking after him. Jesus, I never even knew where the guy lived until you just told me.'
'Two guys?'
'Sure, and I've got bruises where I think my kidneys is situated to prove it.'
'What else aren't you telling me, Hogie?'
'Meet me at Rosco's, yeah?'
'Give me forty-five,' I said, and hung up.

When the phone rang, again, five minutes later, I checked source. Estelle Scriven's name came up on the monitor, so I switched to answer-service. The world was full of guys with missing wives, wives with missing husbands. I didn't want to be the one chasing Estelle Scriven's runaway husband, job to job, city to city, only to come back with the bad news. Maybe, I just didn't want to be the one bringing Estelle Scriven bad news.

I made one call before leaving to meet Hogie.
'Farouk,' I said. 'You free to get over to Rosco's?'
'Right now?'
'That a problem?'
'No problem. What's on, Charley?'
'Maybe, nothing, but I'd just as soon have you watching my back, just in case.'

'You got it'

It was like that with guys who went way back.

I drove down to Venice on sensors. The fog was lifting, but I didn't want the auto-comp giving me a hard time. Traffic was light, and moving steady. It was five before noon when I pushed through the door of Rosco's, on Speedway and Thornton, one block in from Ocean Front Walk and the Venice beach. The place was packed. I eased past the crowd waiting in line at the service-counter and saw Hogie up back at a table for four with one seat untaken. He had his head buried in a plate of eggs easy-over, hash browns, and smoked rashers, crisp as a post-escalation Londoner. The early morning muscle hadn't affected Hogie's appetite, any.

'I kept you a seat, Charley,' Hogie said, as I came over. He kicked out the spare seat with his foot and I sat down.

The two guys sat either side of Hogie at the table had cups of coffee in front of them. One of them was wearing mirror shades and a fluorescent blue sports jacket. The other was a bag of bones, with watery eyes and flared, red nostrils. I recognised the look. With Barbi Doll, there was no cold turkey, just a cold slab in the County Mortuary after the cred ran dry and there were no marks left to bottom-line the next hit. It was the one in the sporty jacket who jammed the gun into my knee-cap.

'Friends of yours?'

'Sorry, Charley. These guys didn't leave me no choice.'

'You got egg on your chin, Hogie,' I said.

The guy with the fatal habit pushed back his chair and stood up. A kid at the table behind turned to complain when his chair got jolted, took a look at what he would be dealing with, and changed his mind.

Smart kid.

'We don't want to rush you,' the guy said.

His partner jabbed the gun hard into my knee. I got the point, and stood up.

'Enjoy your breakfast, Hogie,' I said.

Out on the piazza, a Chevy Dominator with six wheel drive, cattle bars front and back, smoked windows, and tyres with dinosaur's teeth for tread, occupied the square like a Sherman Mark Thirty-Two deliberating on which building it was going to take out first.

The mid-day sun had scorched away the last of the fog. Kids with long hair and beads were setting up their leather goods pitches on the pavement. A guy with his face made up like a clown, carrying a pair of stilts over his shoulder, was heading down Thornton towards the beach and a hard afternoon's work parting out-of-town tourists from their small change.

'Front seat, Charley. Paco, you drive.'

It was the guy in the sports jacket and mirror glasses giving the orders. He now had the gun in full view but nobody, except me, seemed to notice. The gun was a Colt Cremator, and I did like he said.

Paco selected manual transmission, fired the straight-eight, and gunned the Chevy out of the square.

'You want to know why we call him Paco?' the guy in the back said.

'No, but you're going to tell me, anyway.'

'It's Italian — means "a little." Which is exactly what Paco got tucked between his legs.'

I'd heard that laugh before.

When I was visiting an old client in Belleview Sanatorium.

Chapter Six

I first met Farouk over a high-rolling stud poker game in Santa Ana. The local Syndicate operation was calling in a debt, using the gambling table as a laundry, and Farouk came close to blowing the whistle on a two-way dealer, before I was able to warn him off. Tomi Ngsugi, the local Syndicate boss, had hired me for the night to smooth out just that kind of problem. It wasn't my regular line of work but, with the Syndicate, you didn't say no. Farouk was grateful, anyway.

I next ran into him, closer to home, in the Maverick Bar, on Main Street, Santa Monica. He had a two room walk-up above the bar, with a Mexican widow, Felicita Torrés, to cook and tidy up, and was running a regular game in the back room downstairs, making a good living teaching out-of-towners that it wasn't smart to be sitting on a king high bluff, with a thousand green-backs floating in the middle, and him sitting across the table nursing deuces, back to back. When the action was slow, he showed card tricks to the regular hearing-aids.

He was on call for most of the big games around town and, over the years, had fed me useful information when those small-time guys tried to impress with their big-time connections after the cards went cold on them.

Farouk never forgot a favour.

Or, a debt.

I first caught sight of him in the Chevy's wing mirror as Paco turned off Washington Boulevard, at Culver City, and took the slip-road onto the San Diego Freeway. Farouk was driving a red Honda Hiroshima, big job with retractables, and an after-burner that could get up to two hundred interstate. Paco swung north until we hit the Santa Monica Freeway, then floored the pedal.

'You guys should have said we were heading out of town. I'd have brought along an overnight bag.'

From the back, the guy with mirror glasses said, 'Some optimist, Charley.'

We were through Victorville, on Interstate Fifteen, and about to hit the Barstow overpass, when Farouk's Honda torpedoed past the Dominator, then held steady three automobiles and half a mile ahead. After that, he front-tailed the the Dominator, steady as a tic on a blade of grass waiting on the scent of red beef. To the south, the Granite Mountains sat there absorbing the blistering glare of the sun into their black mass. Up ahead, the Mohave Sea spread from horizon to horizon, a highway mirage gone crazy, sand melted to smooth glass by white heat. Only now, there was no sand, just salt water, and any marine life that could handle the toxic count left over from when the Government used to practice popping off big ones out in the desert, and all those experts used to stand around watching, wearing nothing but a pair of dark glasses for protection.

Just ahead of a Terrible Herbst filling station there was a sign that said: 'CHECK YOUR GAS'. Further up, another one, which read: 'DROP TREAD NOW! AFTERBURN ABSOLUTELY PROHIBITED ON ELEVATED SECTION'.

Farouk was already out over the water, on the overpass, heading for Barstow, when Paco swung right, off the highway, onto a dirt track running alongside the water's edge. At the turn-off there was a thirty foot billboard. It said: 'LANDSAKER REALTY DEVELOPMENT', and underneath, in the facsimile of a chicken-scratched afterthought: 'YOU'RE ON THE RIGHT TRACK!' There was an artist's interpretation of a proposed beach-front complex. Blue seas, kids playing in the sand, wind surfers, barbecues throwing up smoke from the back porches of a row of neat little water-front residences, the works. It didn't have a lot to do with the mess of washed up tumbleweed and sun-splintered rock scree that divided the dirt track from the water. Up ahead was parked a Lincoln Dorado Swordfish, its black coachwork gleaming like wet paint in the sun. Whenever life did give a sucker an even break, it usually gave him a Lincoln Dorado Swordfish to go with it, complete with a liveried chauffeur with monogrammed initials sewn onto the breast pocket of his uniform. The chauffeur was waiting beside the Dorado as we pulled up. The monogrammed initials on his breast pocket read: 'JL'. He opened the passenger door and took my arm as I stepped down onto the track.

He said, 'Sir?'

It was an English accent.

What else could you expect?

He was a small guy, and I wasn't ready for the fist that pistoned into my solar plexus, dropping me to my knees in the sand. When I looked up, trying to draw breath into my lungs, he chopped me under the nostrils. Not too hard, but hard enough to hurt like hell. Then he hauled me to my feet and dumped me in the back of the Dorado, hitting the reseal as he closed the door.

I slumped against the leather upholstery, wiping tears from my eyes. After the nausea receded, and my eyes cleared, I looked across at the guy seated the other end of the expanse of button-studded black leather. He was wearing a loud, chocolate brown suite and, on his face, an earnest, nothing to hide expression. The kind they teach young sales executives to wear at weekend training seminars. He looked the kind of guy who always ordered off-menu, but didn't always get it.

'People been taking liberties with me lately, Charley,' he said. 'I didn't want you to be under any illusions.'

'Okay, so now I'm all straightened out. Does Paco drive me back into town, or do I walk?'

'This could go either way, it's up to you.'

'How come I don't lean across and throttle your fat throat?'

He smiled. 'Charley, maybe you don't know it, yet, but you're in a lot of trouble. Could be, I can help out.'

'It would have to be some trouble.'

'I'm looking for Ross Helgstrom.'

'Yeah, I was wondering when that name would come up.'

'You know where I can find him?'

'Go ask the Police Department. They're tracking his plastic, right now.'

'My information is that you work for Helgstrom.'

'Your information is out of date. I quit. Some clients, the price is too high, period.'

The chauffeur was at the rear window of the Dominator, smoking a straight, and talking to the guy with mirror shades through the open window. They were laughing about something. Paco was still in the driver's seat, staring out over the water. I wondered how strung out he was, when he'd cranked his last hit. I got close to a strung out Barbi freak once, when I'd hauled a drop-out kid back to his old man in Pasedena. That was just one more time the price came too high.

'What does "MD Factor" mean to you, Charley?'

'Only, what I read about it in the papers, like everybody else. What is this, a game show?'

'No game, Charley. Let me remind you. Government scientific research project, co-financed with the Japanese, very hush, hush.'

'Yeah, till the research plant, in Pennsylvania, blew up, taking six hundred employees with it.'

'The State Department denied any knowledge of the project.'

'Only, nobody was buying.'

'Right, Charley.'

'So, where is this heading?'

'The MD factor is the point at which molecular density goes critical, inverts to become anti-matter. Like a black hole in space. They were working on creating a black hole in a total environment, controlled laboratory situation. The idea was to find out if they could arrest the process, then reverse it. They were working on miniaturisation, Charley.'

'Yeah, and the whole thing blew up in their faces.'

'Maybe, it did. But, not before the State Department had got busy with all kinds of plans based on the commercial and military implications.'

'We've come a long way from Ross Helgstrom.'

'Not so far as you think, Charley.'

He punched a button on the arm-rest and a drinks tray slid free of the divider behind the chauffeur's seat. He helped himself to an imported mineral water and topped up the glass with perma-cubes. He didn't offer me anything.

'Picture this, Charley,' he said. 'I'm into realty. Have a smart office on Beverly Drive, a good looking secretary who goes down on me once a week, regular as clock-work, despite I'm a fat, ugly bastard.'

The leather-work was decorated with a row of fancy white-lace antimacassars. They were monogrammed, too, just like the chauffeur's jacket pocket.

'JL?' I said. 'You're the Landsaker on the hoarding, figures on developing this waterside waste-dump into prime resort acreage?'

'I heard you were a detective, Charley, and you can call me Jake, just so long as you don't keep interrupting.'

He took a sip of mineral water, then continued. 'I'm playing a round of golf at the Marine and County with a buddy who just happens to be chairman of the State Development Commission. In the members' bar, after I've let him win, but without making it too obvious, he introduces me to some guy in the same line of work, only on a Federal level. You hear what I'm saying?'

'Sure, I hear what you're saying. You're so well connected, how come you need to keep third-rate muscle like those guys on the payroll?'

The chauffeur was through swapping jokes with the guy in the mirror shades, and was down at the water's edge bouncing stones off the water. Paco was still staring out to sea.

'You make enemies, Charley.'

'I can imagine.'

He rode the interjection.

Inter-mesh bathed in transmission fluid.

Jake Landsaker was used to a smooth ride.

'What happens next, is,' he said, 'this guy turns up at my office. He's got two other guys with him.'

'This guy is Ross Helgstrom, right?'

'Right, Charley, and these two other guys are with SISS, that's the Senate Internal Security Sub-Committee.'

'I'm impressed.'

'Me, too, Charley. They're talking buying up low potential acreage at prime rate, plus some. I think I'm dreaming.'

'You were, Jake. So, where does the MD Factor project fit in?'

'They were waving big money, Charley. Why should I be asking questions?' He was silent a moment. Then, he said. 'You remember that big scandal blew up. Non-voluntary relocation of the city zero-cred zones?'

'Sure, I remember. Democrat smear campaign orchestrated by some low-life news editor after the explosion in Pennsylvania

ran out of mileage. It was all over by the midday edition.'
'And the "Dims"?'
'Tabloid-speak for Diminutives. The poor bastards who were due for non-voluntary relocation.'
'Any bells ringing, Charley?'
'If you're saying what I think you're saying, you have to be crazy.'
'It was for real, Charley.'
'Right, Jake.'
'I was flown out to Washington, first class all the way. Suite of rooms at The Sheraton.' Had meets with a lot of guys involved in the project.'
'And you got to meet the President.'
My nose was still hurting. I was tired of the conversation. But there was no right time, right place, to tell a guy he was a sap.
'It was a government contract, minimum finance guarantees, the works,' Landsaker said. 'First ten thousand acreage I bought up, money came through, as promised, no problem.'
'And then?'
'And then I ploughed that money, plus I took on a partner willing to invest, bought up more acreage.'
'And then, Helgstrom disappeared.'
'I rang various numbers I'd been given, nobody'd heard of these guys. I'm in deep Charley.'
'You would have to be. Scam like that would take some outlay. They would have expected a sizeable return on their investment.'
I helped myself to a tumbler and a bottle of Yankee Yell from the hospitality tray. Landsaker didn't object.
'Who did you buy from, Jake?'
'That's what I've been thinking.'
'Only, now, it's too late. Helgstrom rode the headlines to sting you, Jake. It won't be the first time it's happened, but I've got to hand it to the guy. If you're going to lie, make it a big one.'
I finished the bourbon, replaced the tumbler on the drinks tray, and tried the door handle. It was locked. Landsaker pressed another button on his arm-rest and the door came open. The chauffeur reappeared as I got out.
'Okay, Mr Landsaker?'
'Okay, Clem.'

I poked my head back out of the heat into the air-conditioned interior. 'I could offer to find him for you,' I said. 'But, I don't think it would do any good.'

'You get introduced to a guy at the Marine and County, you don't think there's going to be a problem, right?'

'Wrong, Jake,' I said, and started off down the dirt track towards the Interstate.

Landsaker called after me. He was out of the limousine, now, small and insignificant, framed between the Dorado and the Dominator, the desert and the sea. Clem, the chauffeur, was behind him, holding the door.

'You're in the frame, too, Charley,' he said. 'You better remember that.'

I was a quarter of a mile down the track when the Bell PJC appeared, flying in low, over the sea. The PJC is a Police Traffic Department Copter, designed to burn break-downs on the LA Island Freeways, during peak hour traffic. It looked out of place over the water. The copter gained elevation as it approached the parked vehicles. Landsaker and the chauffeur were back in the limo by now. The Chevy Dominator dug dirt, with its massive back treads, and took off down the dirt track in the opposite direction. The PJC hovered, at fifty feet, above the Lincoln Dorado. I could read 'TRAFFIC CONTROL', etched in blue on broad yellow flashes. Then there was a blue flash, a momentary flicker that welded the two machines into one. There was no explosion, no flame, no sound apart from the chop-chop-chop of the rotor arms. When the dark after-image of the laser beam had cleared from my retina, the Dorado was gone.

The PJC boosted its stabilisers and swung around on its own length to face the Dominator which was making fast time behind a smoke-screen of desert dirt. Then, the copter turned through a hundred and eighty degrees and hit forward thrust in my direction. I could make out the pilot and co-pilot through the plastic bubble of the cockpit. They were wearing Police Department regulation issue helmets and mirror glasses.

I started to run.

The chopper blades were carving slices over my head when the thunder of the engine turned into a scream. I hit the ground and rolled down the slope towards the water's edge, getting tangled in the mesquite, elbows dug into the sun-splintered scree. The PJC banked sharply, its rotor arms spinning circles too close to the ground. The plastic bubble shattered and the pilot slumped forward against his safety harness. Blood sprayed the cockpit interior like fresh popped red champagne.

Then one of the rotor arms hit ground zero and the copter cart-wheeled across the track and into the water. This time there was an explosion. And a sheet of flame that boiled the sea around the crashed copter. Chunks of wreckage cut parabolas through the air, charging the shimmering atmosphere with the white heat of flying shrapnel.

I was climbing the embankment when Farouk pulled up in the Honda and got out. He was holding a seven millimetre magnum, four-power scope. The weapon loaded a 148-grain solid state, heat-seek cartridge.

'Tell me I'm wrong, Charley. Did I just off two cops?'

'Why, do you have a problem with that?'

'I don't need the heat.'

'Neither did Jake Landsaker.'

The Chevy Dominator was out of sight, but its dust trail still visible, tail-back drifting out over the sea, ochre mist on steel blue. Farouk raised the hunting rifle to his shoulder, focussed the scope on the apex of the con trail, whispered 'boom', but didn't squeeze the trigger.

'Won this from a hayseed down from Montana, straight played two pair.'

'My lucky night.'

'Luck didn't come into it,' Farouk said.

Then: 'Hey Charley, when it gets so you can't tell the good guys from the bad guys, I'm out of here.'

'You and me both, Farouk,' I said.

Chapter Seven

It was late afternoon when Farouk dropped me off in the piazza out front of Rosco's, in Venice. The kids with long hair and beads had all packed up their wares and gone home. The Santa Ana was blowing in off the ocean, creating twisters of deep-pan pizza boxes, cigarette cartons, and yesterday's late editions in the dust of the parking lot, a living sculpture that went with the mural on the south wall of the square, a surrealistic panoramic of Ocean Front Walk under snow, that had been repainted after the Big One of Ninety-Seven had destroyed the original along with the building it had been painted on. Nobody was complaining about the Santa Ana. It kept the fug inland, allowed the joggers, skaters and trick-cyclists to leave their filter-masks at home...

Most days.

The sun, enlarged by its evening perspective through the curve of the atmosphere, hung above the placid ocean, daring the water to quench its fire. On the streets, shadows were growing longer, tempers growing shorter, as dusk, once again, failed to promise any release from the heat. It was like that in LA Island City, when April began creeping towards May.

'You okay, Charley?'

'I owe you.'

'You don't owe me a thing.'

I declined Farouk's offer of a drink and drove the Pulsar back to Century City, keeping one GO intersection ahead of the peak-hour build-up all the way. Santa Monica Boulevard was a mainline artery about to coagulate, I was a white anti-body, racing for the open wound. I parked in the basement lot underneath my building and took the float up to reception. At the desk, Harry Cohn, the security guy, was sleeping peacefully. On the desk in front of him was a can of Michelob, a half-eaten quarter pounder with everything on, and an early evening racing edition of *The Post*. Harry had slept at that desk for all of the five years I had been stranded in the apartment block. He was a nice old guy, with the occasional reliable tip for the three-thirty at Sunnydale but, right now, reliable tips for the three-thirty at Sunnydale weren't going to help me sleep nights.

I helped myself to the key from the rack without disturbing his five-spread accumulator dreams and rode the float to the tenth floor. In my apartment I showered and changed, built a bourbon, straight up, and threw a cannelloni dinner in the micro. The TV news was all European peace initiatives. I blanked the screen and sat down with my drink to think it all through.

So, okay, Ross Helgstrom was like science.

The more you knew, the less you knew.

Sure, I knew he'd last touched down at Kennedy, sometime around noon yesterday, and was, most likely, way gone from that location, running on delinquent plastic... knew he'd run a scam on Jake Landsaker, an expensive scam, with a lot of serious organisation lined up behind it, but... I didn't know why Landsaker had been whacked by two guys in a Bell PJC Copter... I didn't know why two gunsels had attacked me and Smoky Griscom aboard the *Rosita Recherché*, whether it was intended as a hit, or whether it was me or Smoky they were after... didn't know how come his sister, Daisy Creek, was laying on his carpet with two holes in her back when I went round to check out the apartment, in Palisades, just like he had paid me to do — or, why a crazy, good looking woman, with a sixth dan black belt in martial arts, had been dancing attendance on the corpse.

I didn't know shit.

Some *senei*.

I reached for the phone and put in a call to Weapon Response Assurance Incorporated, the half-baked outfit that handled security for the building.

A girl answered.

Warm lilt to her voice.

Smoothing out any hard edges.
Maybe, Jamaican.
'WRA,' she said. 'How may I help you?'
'Yeah,' I said. 'Would you connect me with whoever is responsible for duty roster allocation?'
'That would be Mrs Keene, sir. Would you hold the line, I'll check she's free?'
Lazy accents on the 'check' and the 'free.'
'Her job may depend on it.'
'May I say who is calling?'
'Detective Stacey, West Hollywood Division.'
Wolfgang 'Wolf' Stacey was Hetty O'Hara's catch partner at the West Hollywood Precinct. Back before Hetty and me became an item, when she was still Precinct House Community Relations Officer at West Hollywood, her and Stacey had had a thing going. It hadn't lasted long. Hetty had described him as fastidious, straight down the line, potentially psychopathic. How else would you describe a guy who made love like he thought he was doing you a favour? I'd had a run-in with Stacey, one time, which was how I met Hetty. I should have been grateful to the guy, but, it still gave me a punch in the gut every time I thought of her and that scud together.
The line clicked, some. That was followed by a prolonged silence before another voice came on the line.
'Mrs Keene speaking. How may I be of assistance?'
All bristles.
'It's more, how can I be of assistance to you, Mrs Keene,' I said. 'We got two kids down here in the holding tank been doing a little research into the efficiency of various security outfits operating in the area, and guess what, your outfit comes bottom of the list. Now, these kids aren't so dumb they don't know an AFTD from a welcome mat reads, by your leave, but they've been making good money passing on the information to wetbacks who don't know any better'
'Wetbacks?'
'That's what I said lady, wetbacks. You have a problem with that?'
'As a matter of fact…'
'As a matter of fact I don't give a…'
'Detective Stacey, would you mind if I call you right back?'

'Call me back? Don't get wise with me, Mrs Keene. You're looking for verification, right? Check out I'm not some sidewalk scumbag pulling a scam? Well, I'll tell you what, I don't have time for all this shit. We got a surveillance running on a made guy over at Studio View, Century City, and we don't want any ass-hole barging in with his list of easy options, blowing the stake. Am I making myself clear, Mrs Keene?'

'Studio View, Century City?'

'That's right, Mrs Keene. You got an old guy down there, sleeping his life away. I want him changed for somebody can handle himself.'

The bristle was still there.

'I'll see what I can do.'

'You'll have to do better than that. Your license to operate will depend on it.'

'Studio View, Century City?'

I felt bad about Harry, but, what the hell.

Maybe, I should have been a cop.

A mean bastard cop just like Wolfgang 'Wolf' Stacey.

'You got it, Mrs Keene,' I said, and hung up.

The micro had switched itself off. I pulled out the cannelloni dinner, took one look, then dumped it in the disposal. Back in the lounge, I checked incomings. Smoky had called. So had Hetty. So had Estelle Scriven, still anxious to have me track down her old man and whatever competition had been up-front enough to run a flank on what she had going for her. I gave her a call and invited her to diner at The Beanery, on Franklin Avenue. I figured that the chilli sauce Manuela Ortiz served up with his tacos would sweat out any guilt I might be feeling at giving her the run-around. Besides, I couldn't imagine any more cred updates would be coming through from Ross Helgstrom, and I was without a client. Estelle Scriven accepted my invitation as if I had just signed a blank cheque and told her she could fill it in any way she wanted.

Then, I called Malloy, at the Santa Monica Precinct.

'Malloy,' I said, 'will you check with Traffic, see if they have an overdue PJC?'

'What kind of question is that?'

'The kind that goes hand in glove with an answer, Patrick.'

I could picture his expression — like a Navaho dirt farmer

had just tried to persuade him that planting corn was a whole lot more fun than chasing buffalo around the prairie on a pony.

'Don't get smart, Charley.'

'Check it out, will you. I'll fill you in when you get back to me.'

'That a promise?'

'That's a promise, Patrick.'

After that, it was Hetty's turn. The desk sergeant at West Hollywood told me she was out on a ten-thirty-nine, a Crime in Progress. I asked, what kind of crime, and the desk sergeant said: 'This district? Most likely some pimp beating up on one of his girls. I shouldn't lose any sleep, Charley.' I thanked him for his advice and left a message saying I was with a new client this evening, she could drop by late, or I would call her in the morning.

I had time to fix another drink before it was my turn to be fielding the calls. It was Eddy 'The Peep', ringing for a pat on the back.

'Have I got some prints for you, Charley?' he said.

'Not me, Eddy, it's Jake Lomax wants the prints.'

'I wouldn't be certain about that, Charley. You wait till you see what I got here. That dame, Petra, sure is some hot stuff.'

'The Westward Chapter of the Secular Order of Creative Celibacy was a blind, just like her old man suspected?'

'You got to be kidding. Every Wednesday night, same motel, same guy... you want to get a look at what's been going down.'

'You and Rita run through the pictures, Eddy, work up some fresh ideas?'

'Rita? Oh, Rita. She's history, Charley. You interested? I can let you have her number.'

'Thanks, but no thanks.'

Why had it got that there were no more surprises, that you were always disappointed, that guys like Eddy 'The Peep' Lagunda could always make a good living confirming everybody else's worst fears.

'Bye, Eddy,' I said.

I'd just decided on a shirt and tie for my dinner date with Estelle Scriven when the phone rang again.

'Yup,' Malloy said. 'Traffic have a copter overdue from the Bell Maintenance Plant at Salt Lake City. Two guys were sent out yesterday to take delivery, but they haven't showed up yet.'

'You can tell Traffic they'll find it half a mile south of the approach elevation to the Barstow Overpass, on Interstate Fifteen. In shallow water, they can't miss it.'

'Tell me more, Charley.'

'Nothing more to tell. Had some business in Barstow, saw it come down from the highway.'

'You were going to level with me, Charley.'

'One more thing. When they recover the bodies, check out if they were the same two guys sent out to take delivery.'

I broke connection, finished the bourbon, and decided against the shirt and tie in favour of the vest I was already wearing.

A little after eight I left my apartment. Downstairs, in reception, a young guy was seated behind the security desk. He had blond hair, a cut-away denim jacket, deep tan, and body tattoos that were like a boa constrictor wrapped around a bronze statue.

'You the new security guy?'

The kid stood up.

'Yes, sir!'

I figured he was six-ten, without sneakers.

'Well, listen good. Nobody, but nobody, goes up to my apartment without you clear it with me first. I'm not home, you send them away. You got that?'

'No problem, Mr...?'

'Charley Case. I'm sixty-two fifteen.'

'You have some ID?'

'What's your name, bud?'

'Craig, sir, Craig Homer.'

'Good to meet you, Craig, you're my kind of security.'

I showed my plastic, wished him a good evening, and went on down to the basement park to pick up the Pulsar.

The Beanery, on Franklin, looked no better, or no worst than any other tacky take-out taco joint in LA Island City. Outside, on the sidewalk, was a holo of a Mexican in sombrero and bandoleers, holding a menu. You could see right through him. Inside, was all earthenware pots and Aztec wall paintings. Along one wall was the usual glass-fronted cooler where you could help yourself to wine or imported beer, and there was a guitarist who came in two nights a week, with a Spanish dancer, who had nice legs, high heels, and a fine pair of castanets. The dancer was nice looking, too.

What made the Beanery special was Manuela Ortiz. The decor, he'd inherited from a previous owner and not changed a thing. How he ran his kitchen was something else. You could get *tacos, tortillas, sambutes, chalupas,* or *enchiladas,* you never got more con than carné, and the corn meal — *masa harina,* as Manny would call it — was pounded into fresh dough right there on the premises. When I arrived, Estelle Scriven was waiting at what passed for a bar, and Manuela Ortiz stepped between me and the smart opening lines I had rehearsed on the drive over.

'Charley! Hey, man, good to see you.'

'You, too, Manny.'

'So, where's my favourite cop tonight, Miss O'Hara working, yeah?'

'Yeah, she's working, Manny.'

'Okay, so I find you a nice quiet table in a corner, someplace.'

'I'm not on my own, Manny. I'm with the lady perched on the bar stool behind you.'

'Hey, why don't you tell me these things?' He turned to include Estelle in the conversation. 'You should have told me you was with Charley, I'd have mixed you one of my special margaritas.'

'I prefer my drinks straight up, no mixer,' Estelle said.

'That's what Charley used to say.'

'So, with you, Manny, I make an exception. Have the margaritas, Estelle, you won't regret it.'

Manny beamed.

'Two margaritas, coming up, Charley.'

Estelle was wearing a loose-fit black trouser suit and red mules. With the light in the right place, you could see her body, silhouetted through the gossamer fabric. Round her neck was a string of rough-cut jade, big chunky stones, no reason to blow cred on a wall safe, but the perfect accompaniment to the black suit and her raven hair, pinned high at the back, accentuating her high cheek bones and those rogue baby-blue eyes.

Manny was busy mixing the drinks.

'So, who's the cop? She something special?'

'Is that important?'

'You never know, Charley.'

Manny brought the drinks, then led us through to a table. It was a small place. There were four couples eating, and two tired out-of-town businessmen, nursing tequilas, and wondering how the hell they got stuck with each other's company for the evening. The guitarist with the nice legs was taking a break. *Vaya Con Dios* was playing on the sound system, but not too loud.
Very romantic.
The two tired businessmen were all eyes for Estelle. I hoped they weren't going to get too drunk on the tequila. I didn't want to have to end the evening hitting one of them.
Or, both.
Manny pulled out our seats and left us with the menu. It was shaped like an Aztec Priest's headgear, with the regular menu printed over the blanked-out face. Today's lunchtime special was still tagged to the side with a clip.
'I'll order, yeah?' I said.
Estelle took the menu out of my hands.
When Manny came back, she asked for the pumpkin flower soup and *panuchos* to follow. 'Beer, okay?' she said, then went over to the wall cooler and came back with two Dos Equis. She didn't ask if I wanted a lime wedge.
'You can tell a man by where he likes to eat.'
'Did I pass?'
'We haven't eaten, yet.'
The soup arrived. It was bright yellow, the yellow a kid would use to paint the sun. Estelle spooned some into her mouth, and said, 'You passed, Charley.'
'So, tell me about your husband, Estelle,' I said.
'Your special cop, Miss O'Hara, do you live together?'
'Listen,' I said, 'I don't want to hurt your feelings, and I can't say I'm not tempted, I'd be crazy not to be, but what goes on between me and Hetty is not what we're here to talk about.'
'Charley...'
'And, I won't say that I'm not flattered, either...'
'Maybe, you're a dollar short on confidence, Charley.'
'You do have a husband?'
She knew I wasn't playing.
When the tears came into her eyes it took me by surprise.
'I haven't been straight with you, Charley.'
'You don't have a husband?'

'I did.'

'You split up, he's behind with the alimony — is that what this is all about?'

'He's dead.'

I could see how much it hurt her to say the word.

'Estelle, I'm sorry…'

'Will you excuse me for just a moment?'

She got up and made her way through the tables to the powder room. The two tired businessmen followed her with their eyes. I wasn't in the mood. I pushed back my chair and went over, leaning in close over their table, so as not to disturb the other customers.

'You undress that lady one more time,' I said, 'I'm going to take you both outside, kick the shit out of you.'

Manny was at our table clearing the soup bowls. He came over.

'Is there a problem, Charley?'

'No problem, Manny.'

The two guys just sat there with their mouths hanging open. After a moment, one of them asked Manny for the tab.

'No offence, mister,' the other one said, as they stood up.

Estelle was gone ten minutes. In the meantime, Manny arrived with the *panuchos*. The *tortillas* were fried and dried just right and the chicken breasts looked like they would melt in the mouth like spiced cream. I stuck with the Dos Equis till Estelle came back.

When she sat down, she said: 'Could we go some place else to talk?'

I waved to Manny and when he came over, gave him my plastic.

'Something wrong with the *panuchos*, Charley.'

'They look too good to eat.'

'You want to order something else?'

'Just the tab, Manny,' I said. 'The lady's not feeling well. We need some air.'

Manny was back inside one minute.

'You've been a good customer, Charley, and I don't want to make a scene.'

He put my plastic back on the table. It had been scorched.

'Delinquent, Charley.'

'You've got to be kidding.'
'I could lose my license.'
'Listen, there's a mistake.'
'Central Comp don't make mistakes. This area, you got to have status, you're off-limits, Charley.'
'I can pay,' Estelle said.
'That don't make no difference. I could get into a lot of trouble, him being in here.'
'Come on, Estelle,' I said, 'Let's get out of here.'
'You know I have to report this, that I had an illegal in here?'
'You do what you have to, Manny.'
'I thought you and this guy were like that,' Estelle said.
'That's how it goes in LA.'
'No hard feelings, Charley?'
'It's okay, Manny.'
'See you again, yeah, once it all gets straightened out.'
'Sure,' I said.

Outside on the sidewalk, I stared at the traffic cruising Franklin, Estelle with her arm through mine, running through all the things I would do to Ross Helgstrom if I ever caught up with him. I had a fresh pack of Heaven's Door in my pocket and half a tank of gas in the Pulsar. It wasn't much in a city where, with cred, you could buy anything, and, without it, you were a big fat zero.

The two tired businessmen were parked just down the block in a hired Ford Fireball, studying a guide-book in the front seat. I knew the auto was a rental because it had red plates. They were curbed in a restricted zone. It was the play with Estelle that had thrown me. A tail would normally stay anonymous, melt in with the scenery.

It was a smart move.

And I was a dumb ass-hole.

'My place, Charley?' Estelle said.
'I don't have a lot of choice.'
'Thanks a bunch.'
'No strings?'
'Only the ones you feel like pulling, Charley.'

Chapter Eight

I spent the night on Estelle Scriven's sofa, despite the two large bourbons chased down with two more large bourbons that she fixed up when we got back to her place in Glendale, despite my total assets no longer included a fresh pack of Heaven's Door, despite Estelle had changed out of her loose fit trouser suit into a loose fit house-coat, with a loose fit belt tied loose at the waist. Maybe, I had a screw that was loose, too, turning down an offer like that...

Estelle fixed breakfast. Eggs sunny-side, corn muffins, tomatoes and bacon. It was a breakfast that went with the house. There should have been kids screaming around, climbing into school uniforms and heading off for the bus. I should have been buttoning a fresh pressed shirt, checking my brief case to see the paperwork was still in alphabetical order, catching the early flight to Syracuse for one more important meeting and, maybe, that cute little courier from the Conference Centre reception who had come on strong last time out. Instead, I washed down my breakfast with a pot of scalding hot coffee, then mixed an OJ Highball, three parts OJ to two parts bourbon. Estelle was wearing the loose fit house-coat, again, but my mind was on other things.

'How was the breakfast, Charley?'

'Something to remember,' I said.

The Ford Fireball, which had followed us out from the basin, was gone. Maybe, the two guys had sat out there all night, maybe they hadn't. It was routine surveillance procedure to call it a day — some day! — at 7a.m. After that, you rotated the team, or picked up later, relying on the surveillance subject's known movements. Across the way, there was an old guy fixing his garden sprinkler. Apart from him, there was nobody on the street. If those guys were going to pick up on my known movements, already, they were one step ahead of me.

In the lounge, I put through a call to Federal Comp Enquiries. They informed me that my cred status had been suspended by Internal Revenue, pending investigation. I asked the guy, what investigation, and, how long was this investigation going to take? He said he was sorry, but, there was nothing more he could do to help, why didn't I try Internal Revenue? Internal Revenue gave me the run around for twenty minutes, then referred me back to Federal Comp. Back with Federal Comp, they bounced me from one department to another before a cute sounding girl told me the local Police Department had been advised of my downgrade status, and that bailiffs from the Sheriff's Office would be around today to confiscate my possessions and advise the building supervisor that my tenancy had been terminated.

I thanked her for her help.

'Glad to be of assistance, sir,' she said.

Federal Comp was hack-proof. In Twenty-Five, the State Commission for Protection of Information had covered all the options. Only the Federal Bureau had 'hostile' input access. I didn't want to think about the Fed's.

'I can help, Charley,' Estelle said.

'If only it was that easy.'

'You know you can stay over, any time you want?'

'I got the picture.'

I backed the Pulsar out of Estelle's driveway and headed back down into the basin. Beverly Hills was a forty minute run. On Beverly Drive there were plenty of vacant parking bays but, without plastic, there didn't seem any sense in not pulling over in the restricted zone right out front of the Landsaker Realty Development Corporation building. Auto-comp advised me to relocate 'to avoid fixed penalty infringement', then told me I was nearly out of gas.

It wasn't the kind of advice I could use.

The Landsaker building was all tubular steel and bronzed glass, with a steeply inclined lawn cut by a flight of steps. There were revolving doors and, in the reception lobby, a bronze statue of a naked kid relieving himself over a pond full of koi carp. The girl behind the desk patted her hair and gave me a bright smile.

'Lovely,' she said.

'You ever heard of Abraham Lincoln?'

'Wasn't he...?'

'It's sometimes better to keep your mouth shut and be thought a fool, than open it and remove all grounds for doubt.'

It was the only quote I knew, but it was a good one.

'The fish.'

'Now, I'm with you. Is Jake around?'

'Mr Landsaker?'

'To you, maybe.'

She patted her hair some more.

'Is Mr Landsaker expecting you?'

'No, but his partner is.'

She was wearing a knitted cardigan over a white blouse that was buttoned all the way to the top. She fingered the top button and my eyes followed hers to where the response alarm was concealed beneath the lip of the desk, on the left.

'Mr Houseman?'

'You got it.'

'And you are...?'

'Tell him "Ross", but that's Mr Helgstrom to you.'

'If you would just excuse me a moment,' she said. Then added: 'I'll check Sam is free.'

It was a closing-seconds touchdown to her, but I consoled myself thinking about her and Jake Landsaker, once a week, regular as clockwork.

She disappeared through a frosted glass swing door leaving me to study the various presentation holo's of development projects that were on display around the reception lobby. Every so often, the holo's slow-faded to a different perspective. Along one wall was a comfortable sofa and a coffee table with a pile of magazines. On top of the pile was a copy of the *National Real Estate Newsletter*. The headline read: 'TAX SHELTER IMAGE, PENDING LEGISLATION DOGS INDUSTRY: BUT STILL BOOMING, EMPHASIS NOW ON DEAL VIABILITY!'

It was a humdinger of a headline and I was still trying to work out what it meant when the receptionist came back through the swing doors.

'Mr Houseman will see you,' she said, 'if you would like to come this way.'

Sam Houseman's office was situated in a corner of the building on the ground floor. It had plenty of space and plenty of light, and looked like it had been ransacked by a brown bear in search of the honey jar. Houseman stood amidst the debris, his collar open at the neck, his tie unknotted and hanging down outside his jacket, a five o'clock shadow around his jaw.

'You're not Helgstrom.'

'You've met Helgstrom?'

'Hey, what the hell is this?'

'This is a way of making sure I would get to see you.'

I looked at the files and storage-disks scattered around the floor, the overturned cabinet, the shattered glass on the framed photograph of Mrs Houseman and the three kids.

'My name is Charley Case,' I said. 'I'm a private investigator, and I've been set up by Helgstrom, just like you. I was hoping you might be able to help me find him.'

'Well, you came to the wrong place, Charley. If I knew where Helgstrom was, I wouldn't have a problem.'

'Don't count on it.'

'Don't count on it? I have to count on it. I got ten thousand acres of precipice in the Santa Monica's, ready to slide first time some guy spits. I got a hundred mile of mesquite and kangaroo rat run along the Mohave Coast. I got twenty miles of perimeter around the downtown zero-cred zone, parking lots and condemned buildings, will be down classified any time. I'm all locked in, Charley.'

Houseman picked up an empty drawer and inserted it back into his desk. Then he started building a pile of files on the desk top.

'I come in this morning, I'm going to get it all straightened out with Jake. What do I find? Jake's playing hookey, no word, no nothing. The building's been broken into overnight. I got a letter from the bank, sitting out in reception, telling me they're calling in the company overdraft facility. One and a half units, right? Two lousy weeks to find one and a half big ones.'

He picked up another desk drawer, then threw it back down. 'Can you believe these guys?' he said. 'It's like they were working from a blueprint. You want to know what the security outfit we use charged us for installations? A fuckin' fortune, that's what, Charley.'

'The cops?'

'Oh, they were impressed, no doubt about it. Outside of that, I've never seen a bunch of guys less interested.'

'You find out what's missing?'

'It will take a while.'

'Ever thought this could tie in with Helgstrom?'

'Only, in my worst nightmares, Charley.'

'What would they have been looking for?'

'Who knows? Title deeds, finance agreements, development contracts, you name it, we kept it all here in the office.'

'So, who were you buying from?'

'I'm not with you?'

'The low yield acreage you got saddled with.'

'I'll move it, Charley, don't go losing any sleep on my account.'

'So?'

It was like somebody close had died. Sam Houseman wasn't yet ready to come to terms with it. He parked himself in the black leather chair behind his desk. 'From all over,' he said. 'There was one outfit in particular, Delta Realty, over on Western. Guy by the name of Clovis. Jake had some special arrangement going with him to cover some of the legwork.'

'Western?'

'Yeah, Western. Dead end location for a realty office, right?'

'You deal with Helgstrom, personally?'

'He came by the office one time with Jake, is all. Jake took care of that end of things.'

'What was he like?'

'Charmer. Knew all the right buttons to press. I didn't like him.'

He sat silent a moment, maybe contemplating just *how* much he didn't like Ross Helgstrom.

'You saw the holo's out in reception,' he said. 'Strictly up-mobile purchaser potential. Real class. There isn't one heat sensitised faucet built into any one of those blueprints wasn't, first, referred to VALS for approval.'

'VALS?'

'The Stanford Institute, Values and Life-styles marketing system. Best consumer research cred can buy. You want to see the bill those guys sent in, and you know what? Those guys don't have a hope in hell of getting paid. Those holo's, that's *all* they are, Charley, just an illusion. I'm up to here in hock, buying into this outfit. I'm on a twenty-five percent cut. We have development approval, we have the finance. It's all looking good. Then, suddenly, Jake takes off at a tangent, chasing down some crazy government project, tying up all the capital in zero potential acreage.'

'It wasn't the government deal that attracted you in the first place?'

'No way. That came after.'

'You had no say?'

'I'm the junior partner, right. Besides, the deal looked good. Why should I complain?'

'And now Jake Landsaker has disappeared?'

'Disappeared? Well, that's not the way I would put it, exactly. Maybe, his car broke down. Maybe, he has a bad hangover, who knows?'

'Yeah,' I said, 'and, maybe, there's a fat Treasury Department cheque in the mail to you, right now.'

Houseman sat back in his chair. The energy was draining out of him as I watched. He looked up at me.

'We're talking white Christmas in LA Island City, right?'

'Looks that way.'

It also looked like a scam within a scam, or, that Landsaker and Helgstrom were in it together, with Houseman as the trick for turning. Lower budget, faster turn around. Except that Landsaker was dead, and the weight on my back hadn't been put there by any team working the sting — no matter how smooth the operation.

The phone rang. Houseman looked at it for a while before picking up the receiver. 'Yeah... right... well, you better put him through.' He covered the receiver.

'First National,' he said, 'pass me my loaded Luger, will you.'

Houseman was a man you could grow to like.

I shouldn't have had to feel sorry for him.

From the door I said, 'It has to get worse before it gets better.'

Houseman smiled. 'Thanks, Charley. You find that bastard, let me know, will you?' Then, into the phone: 'Mr Coppola, hi! Right... I was about to call you.'

In the lobby, the receptionist was on the phone to a girlfriend. She was still fingering her top button.

Through the plate glass I could see a black and white parked up front of the Pulsar. One cop was standing there with his hands on his hips. His partner was checking the VU in the cruiser, waiting for the MD to come back with a make on my licence plate.

The receptionist broke off her conversation.

'I think you got a ticket.'

'Enjoy,' I said.

I went down the steps and turned left towards Will Rogers Plaza. Up ahead, a white Caddy Countdown was parked at the curb, its engine running. As I drew level, the guy at the wheel reached over and opened the passenger door.

It was a perfect play. All I had to do was slide into the seat alongside him and all my troubles were over. Maybe I would get a bullet in the brain. Or, maybe I would get a chance to explain I had nothing to do with Helgstrom, that all I wanted was to get these guys off my back, go home, and catch up on how the Dodgers were making out on the TV.

The black thunderball that exploded from the passenger seat of the Cadillac was a German Rottweiler. Ears chopped to points, the way they do to make them that much more pissed with life. I threw up my arm and teeth bit deep into my fore-arm, ripping jacket fabric and muscle tissue. We hit the sidewalk hard with the dog on top. There was the pressure of jaw clamped to bone, but no pain, not yet. I grabbed for an ear, twisting, pulling away from me, and brought my knee up into the animal's crutch. It released its grip to howl then came at me again. The guy at the wheel engaged first, pulled the passenger door shut as he shot away from the curb. The Rottweiler looked from me to the disappearing limousine, then took off down the road after it.

It had only taken a split second, the time it took for the Caddy Countdown's stop lights to flash once, as the driver hit the brakes then burned rubber in a hard right-hand turn into Carmelita.

I climbed to my feet. My fore-arm was a mess of blood and saliva. The pain was starting to come. First the warmth and then the fire. There was a low brick wall that fronted an office building with people at the windows, watching. Using my good arm,

I peeled off my jacket and sat down on the wall. The patrol car and the cops had disappeared. My Pulsar sat, unattended, outside the Landsaker building. The receptionist was running up the steps and into the building. Maybe it was her who called the medics. I was still sitting on the low brick wall when the ambulance pulled up and cut the siren.

'Okay, bud, just take it easy, yeah?'

Confused.

Thinking it would be a shame, those two guys in their smart white tunics, me all covered with blood, maybe they didn't ought to get too close.

They helped me into the ambulance and got me laid out on one of the two emergency treatment cots. One of the medics fixed up a transfusion drip while the other one ripped the arm off my shirt, skin-popped an anaesthetic, and sprayed the wound with a sterilising agent. I got a good look at the torn flesh and exposed muscle and felt like throwing up.

That wasn't my arm.

It was some other poor bastard's.

The medic found a vein above the wound and sank in a needle. 'That will take care of the cyanosis,' he said. 'Shock is one hell of a defence mechanism but it can also precipitate fatality.' He had a tape running in his top pocket, and a tie-mic clipped to the lapel of his jacket. He probed my fore-arm. I felt cold, tired, the fire receding. 'Multiple peripheral epidermal laceration, deep penetrating wound site, radius and vulna exposed, no arterial rupture — you can count yourself lucky there, bud. Surrounding capillaries dispersed, severe ecchymosis already apparent.' He smiled down at me, 'Ecchymosis... heavy bruising.'

The other medic had carried my jacket through to the cab and was going through the pockets for my billfold and plastic. 'I don't find no ID,' he called back, 'maybe, in your back pocket, mister?'

Then he found the scorched plastic.

'What the fuck?! Hey, Joe,' he said, 'the guy's delinquent.'

'No shit!'

Joe quit probing and switched off his tape. Then he disconnected the drip-feed from my arm. His partner came back through with my jacket and the two of them helped me off the cot and out onto the road. Joe handed me my jacket.

'You got a nerve,' he said. 'What the hell you doing in this neighbourhood, anyway?'

'Fuckin' front of the guy,' his partner said.

Both nodding their heads.

'No wonder the fuckin' hound went for him.'

'Smart mutt!'

They secured the rear doors and climbed into the cab. In tall red letters, on the back of the ambulance, it read: 'THANKS FOR MAKING SPACE, PAL!' The driver hit the siren one time before they drove off.

There was a call box a hundred yards up the street.

I took my time and made it without passing out. Inside the booth, I dialled the operator and asked for a call collect to Malloy at the Santa Monica Precinct House.

'Certainly, sir,' the operator said, 'would you please address your card to the input provided.'

'Maybe you misheard me, I said call collect.'

'Yes, I did hear what you said, sir. But, we still require record of comp verification before I can put you through.'

The booth tilted, then righted itself. There was blood on the floor and on my shoes. A woman strolled up to the booth, looked at me, and hurried away quickly.

'My plastic was stolen, that's why I'm calling the police.'

'If you have a number, I can verify this end.'

'No, I don't have a number.'

'I'm sorry...'

'Don't ever say that unless you mean it.'

'...but in the general interest of our subscribers we are obliged to take all necessary precautions to avoid delinquent abuse of our service. These regulations are in your interest, sir. Please do call again later when you are able to provide verification of your cred status. Have a nice day.'

The line went dead.

I don't know how long he had been standing there.

The kid outside the booth.

Standing there watching me hanging on to the receiver, waiting on the static silence.

He was young, early twenties, with long platinum hair, red T-shirt, red track-suit pants and ski boots. Round his neck was a bead necklace and hanging from the necklace was a photo-portrait of an old guy with a grey beard. The kid had a beard too, only it was blond and might just as well not have been there.

I pushed open the door of the booth and the kid stepped back a pace.

'You think I'm in any condition to hurt you?'

'You meet some, mister.'

'Well, I can't argue with that.'

I was still holding the receiver.

'You on hold?'

'Playing make-believe, kid.'

The kid stepped forward, took the receiver from my hand, held it to his ear.

'You got nothing.'

He recradled the receiver.

'Listen, mister, you want some help, all you have to do is ask.'

'That simple?'

'You want to think about it till you bleed to death?'

'That's not such a bad idea.'

'You're screwy, mister, you know that? Who're you trying to call?'

'You have plastic?'

'Oh, come on!' Then, 'So, all right, now I get it.'

'It's not a long story…'

'I don't need to know, okay?'

' … but, it is complicated.'

'Save it,' the kid said.

He had a money belt strapped around his waist beneath the red T-shirt. He pulled out his ID card and said, 'You want I should make the connection?'

'You're all right, kid.'

I gave him the Santa Monica Precinct number. He fed in his plastic, punched the digits, and handed me the receiver.

Halloran was on the line.

'Thanks, kid. Now push off, will you?'

'You're not so tough, you know that?'

He waited outside the booth while I spoke to Halloran. Halloran told me Malloy was over at the Court House all morning giving police evidence. Murder One, State versus Berlusconi, defence pleading 'diminished responsibility' on the grounds of nobody in his right mind kills the guy downstairs with a kitchen knife on account of the guy's wife wakes up the whole building every time he puts it to her...

Which is every night.

Same time.

You could set your watch by it.

'I don't need this, Halloran,' I said.

I didn't need Detective Third Grade Theo Lipztic, either.

'Long time no call, Charley. I was beginning to worry.'

'You want to put me back to Halloran?'

'Jesus, no. Single handed you made the whole trip worthwhile.'

'In that case, maybe you owe me.'

'Shoot, Charley.'

'You're a smart cop, Theo, you will already have checked out your incoming source monitor...'

'Sure, you're calling from a public booth, Beverly Drive, up by the junction with Carmelita...'

'Right.'

'... and comp verification tells me your name is Ralph Jerome Hutton, address — the hell is this? — Rajneeshpuram, Oregon, on the 218.'

'Which is the guy loaned me his plastic.'

'How come, Charley?'

'You take a while, Theo.'

'Hold, will you?' He was off-line just long enough to key my name into his desk-top input. 'You come back delinquent, Charley, what do you know?'

'And Beverly is a restricted zone, right. According to the Federal Status Protection Act, Twenty-Five, that could get me one to five.'

'You want *me* to come down arrest you, is that what you're saying. You're out of jurisdiction, Charley. What the hell is wrong with the local cops, you want arresting so damn much?'

'I get edgy around strangers.'

'There has to be a catch.'

'Sure, there's a catch, Theo. The catch is I'm bleeding to death all over the sidewalk.'

'You hurt?'

'Just make it quick, will you.'

'Fuck you, Case, I'll bring the medics, right.'

The kid helped me out of the booth.

'You look in bad shape, mister.'

I was leaning heavily on his shoulder. There was another earth tremor, but the kid didn't seem to notice.

'What kind of address is that, "Rajneeshpuram?" You some kind of Jesus Freak?'

'After our founder, the Bhagwan Shree Rajneesh.'

'I've got a lot to thank you for, Ralph.'

'You don't have to thank me. As the Awakened One said: "I am just the finger pointing at the moon. Look at the moon, not the finger".'

'I'll remember that.'

A black and white pulled into the curb and two cops got out. One of them was carrying a baton, Mondanock P31, two-foot long, solid aluminium, the other, a Taser gun, which delivered a fifty thousand volt electronic dart. 'Get out of here, kid!' I shouted. I was already falling as he moved away towards the cop with the baton. The cop swung from the shoulder and caught the kid on the side of his head, sending him sprawling into the road. I was on the ground. The other cop pointed the Taser into my stomach and pulled the trigger. I rotated in free-fall. The razor-sharp edge of pain exploded into a glowing warmth as the old guru raise his finger, pointed towards the moon. Then the moon turned its dark side towards me and the stars went out, one by one, leaving nothing.

Chapter Nine

One time, on a clear day — which even back then didn't occur too often — you could pick out downtown LA from any elevated freeway around the city. Downtown was where the serious money hung out, the commercial heart of a sprawling four thousand square miles of low-rise clapboard suburb that called itself a city. Downtown was loud-mouthed, dirty, and dangerous after dark, but it had something the rest of the basin didn't have...

It had skyscrapers.

Just like Chicago.

Just like Manhattan Island.

Built on multi-national funding and a blind faith in contemporary anti-quake design technology, those high-rise buildings were an innovation to the landscape, rearing up against the skyline, a dark crystalline volcanic upthrust, proclaiming to the rest of Los Angeles City: *This Is Where It's At, Baby!* A vast army of telephone receptionists, secretaries, word process clerks — the day to day grafters holding down unglamorous jobs in a city of illusion and stretch limousines — thought they were untouchable, found themselves nursing dark fantasies of how one day, the sooner the better, they would watch from the sky while all those so called celebrities, those coke-head soap stars, paedophile movie producers, and rock and roll weirdos, along with their exclusive beach-front colony at Malibu, got swallowed up beneath thirty feet of liquid sand — just like the way it happened in the Alaskan quake of Nineteen Sixty-Four.

But that was before the Big One of Ninety-Seven.

Before Valencia Gap cracked open along the Garlock Fault and the Pacific Ocean flooded into Nevada. Before The White House, obliged to accept handouts from all around the world on behalf of its stricken West Coast, pressured the geo-scientists into finally coming up with a solution. Before the body bags got counted and burned, the pyre throwing up a plume of black smoke that could be seen all the way to Tucson, Arizona.

California used to mean 'The Emerald Isle,' and that was how it turned out for Los Angeles City. All those jokes about how California was, one day, going to fall into the Pacific Ocean, those wall murals and paintings showing fancy beach resorts along the Nevada coast-line — only, it was no joke — and California got to have the last laugh.

Despite the body count.

It took LA Island City five years to pick itself up, dust itself down, and start all over again. As a lasting memorial to the dead, the city planners stuck with the old street names, but Downtown, they went one stage further, rebuilding an exact replica of the way it used to be, forgetting that Los Angelinos, no matter what shit hit the fan, just weren't interested in last year's model. The serious money decentralised, electing to go with the new high-rise complexes that were reaching up all over to take a peek over the Sierras. Downtown stayed empty until a new generation of users, abusers, winos and down-and-outs came drifting in, turning the place from a ghost town into a black hole where faded aspirations got sucked in, went anti-matter, and, once in a while, teased the mind like an actor's name nobody could quite remember.

They were singing *Abide With Me*. A group of Salvation Army diehards, two of them holding UV Scatterguns, keeping the dead-beats back from the soup kitchen till they were through singing hymns. Beethoven was staring out over the tangled undergrowth of Pershing Square, looking towards the Philharmonic Auditorium, his face a stone mask of disapproval, decorated with guano.

I was on the corner of Hill Street and Fifth. A kid in a denim jacket, with cut-away sleeves, was pulling at my sneakers, trying to get them off my feet without undoing the laces. Another kid was standing over me, going through my billfold.

He saw that I was conscious.

'Welcome to the zone, bud,' he said.

I kicked at the kid who was worrying my feet.

The kid standing over me kicked me in the ribs. It didn't hurt any more than I was already hurting.

'You're in no condition, mister. Why fight it?'

The other kid had a blade out now, and was slicing through the laces of one shoe. He looked up at me and smiled. 'You think you're going to be needing these?'

The anaesthetic had worn off. There was no place to run from the hurt. One sneaker was gone, and the kid was working on the other one. His partner pinned my arm with his boot and kicked me in the head.

Somebody screamed.

Maybe it was me.

The sky above Pershing Square was a rectangular block... solid... descending. It grew smaller, gained luminosity, a right-angled full moon, but with no bearded guru to point the finger. There were voices. Hetty saying, 'Love can take you only so far,' then Estelle Scriven, her long raven hair wound tight round my throat, 'I'll get the tab, Charley, but, don't forget, you owe me...' The kid with the beads was there, too, dressed all in white, shooting up between his toes, turning red, blood rising through his body like wine fills a glass. He smiled, 'Look me up, sometime, Rajneeshpuram, Oregon, on 218.' Then exploded. 'These birds don't stack easy,' Ross Helgstrom, said. 'One hell of a scam...'

'Charley?'

The Bell PJC Copter came out of the sun, hovered above me, the pilot with his thumb on the *Burn* button. 'You get introduced at the Marine and County, you don't figure there's going to be a problem, right?' Jake Landsaker dissolved in a spread of white heat. A silhouette stood out against the rectangle of white light, them moved away, became a face.

A man and a woman were talking.

Too soft for me to catch what they were saying.

Then a door closed and Travesty Coombe-Lately was looking down at me.

'You're supposed to say "Where am I?"'

'I'll leave the one-liners to you.'

My arm was outside the sheets, the wound a jagged pencil-thin line of red beneath a faint sheen of epidermiseal. There were

no drips, no life supports. I felt good all over.
'You've got some constitution, Charley.'
'It goes with clean living.'
'You came close, you know that?'
'How close?'
'Our medics reckon, without those guys picked you up on Beverly…'
'Our medics?'
'This one's on The Government, Charley.'
'You're with the Bureau?'
'In one, Charley.'
'Why me?'
'Why did we pull you out of a jam?'
'No, why did you drop me in one?'
'You don't know just how lucky, Charley. You're mixing in something goes all the way to the top. We figured zeroing your status would turn the trick. Next thing, you're at Landsaker's office, snooping around. That's when you picked up an XPD upgrade.'
'XPD?'
'Expedite.'
'You mean, whack me?'
'Too right, Charley.'
'The fuckin' hound dog?'
'No way. Ours were the two cops out front of the building. The mutt was with Helgstrom, or so we figured. We also figured that if Helgstrom wanted you gone, it might be an idea to keep you alive.'
'Bait.'
'In one, again, Charley.'
A nurse poked her head round the door, said: 'Sorry, Commander,' and disappeared.
'So, why should the Fed's be so interested in a low-life property scam?'
'What you don't know can't hurt you, Charley.'
'I don't buy any of this.'
'You got a choice?'
'I'm working on it.'
'Don't get too cute, your next reclassification could be for keeps.'

'Don't lose any sleep.'
'Sounds like it could be fun.'
'We had this conversation before.'
'You're slow catching on, Charley.'

She leaned over the bed, covered my mouth with hers, playing games, her tongue with mine. When she was through, I said, 'Did you kill Daisy Creek?'

'What do you think?'

'I think you wouldn't have bothered with the two slugs.'

'In one, again, Charley,' she said.

It was the two tired businessmen from Manuela Ortiz's Beanery who dropped me off out front of Delta Realty, on Western.

'So, you two guys found your way back into town, okay.'

'It's just a job,' the guy driving said.

'How was the wetback?'

That was the other one, from the back seat.

'I was thinking of you, stuck out there at the curb all night.'

'Hot shit, I bet ya.'

'You're never going to find out, fuck-head.'

'Leave it, Mel, will you?'

'Your partner's offering you some good advice, Mel,' I said. 'You ought to take it.'

I got out, slamming the door, and the Fireball was immediately lost in the traffic.

Delta Realty was sandwiched between a gay singles bar called Davida's, and a pizza parlour. They were both open, doing good business, bright lights, music, people coming and going. Delta Realty was boarded up, with no lights showing. I tried the night bell, waited a while, then tried the door handle. It wasn't locked. Inside, there was enough light from the street to see the place had been vacated in a hurry. There were three desks with the drawers hanging open, paperwork on the floor, a filing cabinet with nothing in it. I checked one of the phones. They were still connected. Bass frequencies were pumping through the wall from the bar next door.

I closed the door to the street and found a light switch. Behind the furthest desk was another door, framed glass. A sign on the glass read: 'NATHAN CLOVIS, GENERAL MANAGER'.

I pushed through the door.

The guy in the back room was sat behind a desk, bound to a swivel chair. He wasn't gagged. That was how somebody had been able to put a gun in his mouth and blow his brains all over the wall.

Travesty had said: 'What would you have done, Charley, after you drew a blank with Houseman?'

So I went ahead and dug myself a hole.

A hole deep enough to bury me and Nathan Clovis both.

'I got what I wanted, a source Landsaker was buying his acreage. Outfit called Delta Realty.'

'Slow, muddy water.'

'Yeah, and it also means a triangular configuration, with Helgstrom in the third corner. How else would they work the scam?'

'You'll want this, Charley.'

Travesty Coombe-Lately held a piece of plastic with my name on it. Scorch-free. Viable.

'What are you saying, Travesty?'

'I'm saying you should pick up right where you left off.'

'You guys want Helgstrom so bad...'

'We're not involved, Charley, and that's how it has got to stay.'

'I have a day rate, plus expenses.'

'You also have no option, Charley.'

The worst thing was, the guy had been wearing a toupee. Long, wavy chestnut brown hair. It was lying at the base of the wall. On the wall was a large scale street plan of LA Island City.

Only, now, it looked like a painting by Jackson Pollock.

I went through the guy's pockets, found a wallet, only to confirm it was Nathan Clovis.

Then I went back through to the outer office and called a cab.

Chapter Ten

I had lost two days at the Fed Medic Center. The way my days had been shaking out lately that was no bad thing. It was a quarter after midnight, early Sunday morning, when the cab driver — old Chinese guy, used to be big in martial arts movies till droids and comp graphics threw him out of a job... I got the whole story in seven blocks — dropped me off outside of my apartment building on Galaxy.

Just paid, or not, to everybody else it was a Saturday night. Kids were cruising, hookers hustling, couples riding fancy limousines between high-class restaurants and low-life clubs, maybe doing a couple of lines on the back seat just to convince themselves that they weren't getting any older. Me, I was still in warp space, working on what Friday night had to offer.

'Thought the face was familiar,' I said to the cabby, passing him my brand new plastic.

The cabby smiled.

'Bullshit,' he said, 'but, thanks anyway.'

In reception, Craig Homer was at his desk flicking through a comic book. On the cover was a hunk of meat in a skin-suit kicking all kinds of shit out of an alien. He put the comic down as I came in. 'Mr Case, how goes it?'

'So where was Superman in Ninety-seven, when we needed him?'

'Huh?'

'Don't lose any sleep, kid. You ever see that old black and white movie, "The Lost Weekend"?'

'Black and white? Way before my time, sir.'

'No matter. I've just been on one of those lost weekends, only it came a day early and the bugs crawling out of the plasterwork were for real.'

Craig Homer smiled.

How else was he supposed to respond?

'You had a visitor Thursday night. Miss O'Hara?' he said.

No mention of the Sheriff's Office bailiffs descending on my apartment, hauling out all my furniture, then hauling it all back in again.

'And?'

'I followed your instruction, sir. Told her nobody was to go up to your apartment without specific clearance from you.'

'And?'

'Miss O'Hara told me you had said to come on over and I told her, "I'm sorry, I have no knowledge of that".'

'What time was this?'

'Around two-thirty a.m.. She didn't take it very well, sir. I feel she was of the opinion that your instruction should not have applied to her. I pointed out that, in your absence, there was nothing I could do to help.'

'Thanks a bundle, pal.'

I turned towards the float elevator but Craig wasn't through with me yet.

'Your Pulsar, sir,' he said. 'Recovery people brought it in around five-fifteen. It's in the basement park. You have a breakdown?'

'Yeah, I took a swing at the auto-comp for asking too damn many questions.'

'I didn't ...'

'Sorry, kid, that was out of line.'

'I don't dent easy.'

'That, I can believe, Craig.'

In my apartment the telephone was ringing. It was Eddy 'The Peep' Lagunda.

'You know what time it is, Eddy?'

'Sure I know what time it is. I've been trying to reach you for two days. Where you been, Charley?'

'I told you, you wouldn't believe me.'

'You're going to have trouble believing this, too, Charley. The Lomax prints, right?'

'I'm going to hang up now, Eddy, okay?'

'No, hear me out. The guy his wife, Petra, was screwing, you're never going to believe.'

'Believe me, you're right, Eddy.'

'Jake Lomax.'

'What about Jake Lomax?'

'Guy she was screwing every Wednesday night, hour-rate joint on Fairfax. You believe the guy. Hires a PI to shoot film of him getting on down with his own wife.'

'Just so long as he catches the tab, Eddy.'

'I go round the Lomax place, the personal touch, you know, Charley.'

'You've seen her in action, right.'

'Can you blame a guy for trying? Only, was I to know Jake has taken a day off from the killing floor? Petra starts screaming. The guy starts screaming. All hell breaks loose, Charley. And for why?'

'You're the PI, Eddy,' I said. 'You work it out.'

And hung up.

The phone listed twelve incomings. Over forty-eight hours, not a lot for a guy liked to consider himself patched into the LAI network. I could go ex-directory and maybe half a dozen people would notice.

Eddy was listed four times, Hetty, too. Plus there were two from Estelle, one from Smoky, one from Malloy.

I tried Hetty at the West Hollywood Precinct and was told she was working the eight to four, why didn't I call back then? I got through to the answerphone in her Venice apartment. The recorded message said: 'At the tone leave your name and number, I'll get back to you... unless that's you, Charley, in which case don't hold your breath.'

After that, I said hello to the Jack Daniels, peeled off some of my clothes and went to bed.

When you are living a nightmare there is no need for dreams. I slept ten empty hours of what death must be like if neither heaven or hell come to stake a claim. It was just past noon. The phone was ringing. Like a fool I picked it up.

'Charley?'

'Estelle. You sound surprised.'

'I didn't know where else to try. It was a thousand to one shot.'

'My cred status is all cleaned up. Some bug in the system.'

'You have to be joking.'

'So how come I don't hear you laughing?' I reached over to the bedside table, flamed a Heaven's Door, and waited.

Estelle wasn't a woman to disappoint any man.

'Charley,' she said. 'I wasn't straight with you the other night at Manny's.'

'You weren't straight with me that first night either, Estelle. That makes two nights out of two. You got one good reason why I should take anything you are about to say seriously?'

'I told you my husband was dead.'

'Second night in, right.'

'That melt-down, MD project, Pennsylvania Research Project, you must have heard about it, it was all over the papers.'

'Oh, shit!'

'Charley, my husband, Danny, he was working on that project.'

'Don't tell me, Estelle. The next name out of the hat is Ross Helgstrom, am I right?'

'No, Charley, the next name out of the hat is Nimrod. Washington think-tank set up to explore all the options on the MD experiments.'

If the Feds hoped I would lead them to Ross Helgstrom then I had to assume there was an intercept on my phone line. 'What you don't know can't hurt you,' Travesty had said to me. I wondered just how long it would take for the Fed Analysis Comp to scream *Activate*, and how long after that it would take for my status to be re-upgraded to XPD.

It was like trying to figure how long a spark took to jump a plug gap.

'Estelle,' I said. 'The fun way to do it is this. You ease the barrel of a Colt Cremator into my stupid wide-open mouth till the muzzle rests snug up against my tonsils. Then you whisper "Sweet dreams, baby," and squeeze the trigger.'

I cradled the phone, rolled out of bed and climbed into yesterday's clothes. I figured yesterday's clothes were the perfect cut for going through the whole damn thing again. In a recess, underneath a pile of old shoes in the hanging wardrobe, I dug out the Armstrong Armlite and two clips of ammunition. While I loaded the Armlite I keyed 'NIMROD' in to the comp.

On the VU screen it said:

'NIMROD: Great hunter or sportsman (Bib. ref. GEN. 10.8.9.).
Pop. Usage: Neo-Psycho perfectionist to the point of pedantic, with inability to countenance ineffectuality in self or others.'

Just the kind of guy you would want along on a night out with the boys. The comp queried a read-out on Genesis, chapter ten, verse eight, line nine. I left the query hanging on the VU screen, whispered 'Amen', and slid out into the corridor. Sunlight splintered through the venetians in the passageway. The whine of the float elevator cut through the silence of a mid-day apartment block where everybody was out making an honest living. The pitch of the whine told me somebody was coming up. I loaded a round into the Armlite and held it, two fisted, into the empty cavity of the float shaft. The whine changed note, shifting down a gear. Whoever it was had got out on the floor below. I tucked the Armlite into my inside jacket pocket and ran back down the corridor to the service elevator and stabbed the call button. It took an age for the bell to ring and the doors to open. I backed in and it took another age for the doors to close. Then I pressed my face up close to the audio/response and whispered, 'Basement.'

Craig Homer was waiting for me downstairs. He was holding a Winchester Pump-Action and had his butt parked against the chrome-work of a Buick Microburst. The Buick Microburst had cream fairing, lime-green paintwork and white-walled tyres. It went with his tattoos. The doors of the service elevator, waiting too long for further instruction, began to close. Craig didn't like that one bit, rode both hammers, and left me staring into eternity. A Winchester Pump-Action can take out bricks in a wall, one by one, at fifty feet. The closing doors of the service elevator offered the sanctuary of a coffin.

I shouted 'Hold!' and the doors slid back open.

'Go ahead, Craig, both barrels,' I said. 'I deserve all I get for not having figured you for a Fed plant.'

'Don't go too hard on yourself, Mr Case. Lot of guys, they wouldn't have gotten this far.'

The whine of the float elevator started up again.

Descending.

Spook stepped out of the elevator onto the hard concrete of the basement park. He was wearing a black silicon suit just like the one he had on when I cold cocked him aboard Smoky's *Rosita Recherché* four long days ago. I knew a guy, once, only wore black socks. That way he had no problem making a matching pair when they came back from the laundry. Maybe Spook was like that with Silicon suits.

'You guys are starting to make me feel like my whole life was one big mistake.'

Craig Homer was five yards in front of me, Spook fifteen yards away, on my right flank, along the passageway created between the first row of parked cars and the wall, silhouetted in the light of the float elevator at his back. On the wall, black print on day-glow yellow, a sign read: 'NO OVERNIGHT PARKING FOR NON-RESIDENTS'. I eased forward hoping to cut their line of fire. Looking to reduce the distance between myself, the parked cars, and possible sanctuary. Any small advantage to lessen the odds that were stacking up on me like 897's running out of high octane over Kennedy International on a foggy night in December.

'Not another inch, Mr Case,' Craig said.

'Watch him, sir,' Spook called from across by the float elevator. 'He's better than he looks.'

'Spook,' I said, 'I should have dumped you in the Marina when I had the chance.'

'Yeah, but you blew it.'

'Next time, I'll play it differently.'

'Next time, Mr Case?' Craig Homer said.

'Let's get this over.'

That was Spook.

There was movement behind the driver's wheel of the Buick Microburst. Broad shoulders. Stooped low. Like somebody in the act of hot-wiring the limo. Craig Homer, from where he had his butt parked against the hood of the Buick, couldn't see. Neither could Spook. The straight-eight turbo fed engine thundered into life and the limo hurtled forward rolling Craig Homer along the paintwork. He went down hard, face first, the barrel of the Winchester Pump-Action between his face and the concrete. Blood spurted from his nose. The front fender of the Buick smashed into a row of parked cars, dug for reverse, then burnt rubber, heading backwards in a crazy curve. Spook's fingers clawed beneath his smart-cut black silicon suit jacket but he was never going to make it. The passenger window of the Buick Microburst exploded in a jet of white flame. From out of the flying glass shards a finger of heat prodded Spook in the chest. He fell over backwards then climbed back to his feet. His suit jacket was on fire around a black cauterised hole. Nobody in that condition should have been able to come back for more, but Spook did — and this time he had the Colt Cremator clear of his jacket. The Buick screamed round in a tight circle. A second dagger of white lightning lifted Spook off his feet and dumped him into the open cavity of the float elevator. He hung there, motionless, surrounded by globules of scorched haemoglobin, ruby thought-bubbles too small to be ever able to make it to a single concrete idea.

As Craig Homer sat up I had the muzzle of the Armstrong Armlite pressed into the base of his neck.

'You look a mess, Craig,' I said.

His shirt was ripped, revealing more tattoos on his chest. One of them read: 'MOTHER MADE ME WHAT I AM'. I grabbed the Winchester Pump-Action as the Buick coasted up alongside us and the passenger door swung open. 'Don't be too hard on yourself,' I said to Craig, and swung the barrel of the Winchester against the side of his head.

'Will ya get the fuck in, Charley.'

I had never thought it possible there would be an occasion when I would be pleased to see Hogie Corcoran. But I had been wrong about just about everything else so far — why exclude Hogie.

'Don't think this lets you off the hook, Hogie,' I said. 'You still owe plenty, setting me up with Ross Helgstrom.'

'Charley, have a heart, will ya,' Hogie said, gunning the Buick towards the exit ramp and the sun-soaked coagulated traffic on Galaxy.

Chapter Eleven

Hogie Corcoran had made his five minutes of fame back in Fifty-One when he had been convicted on all counts for conspiracy to breaking and entry, unlawful confinement, possession of fire arms without a permit, assault, and armed robbery. He was convicted because, along with three other low-life sleazes from Venice Beach, Hogie had attempted to rob the First National Bank, on Wilshire, of the three quarters of a million dollars in cash that another sleaze, they met out at the race track, had assured them was being held in the vaults on the account of Coke International for cash payment to its Haitian distributors.

The idea for the heist came from a late night movie on the television. That's how dumb these guys were. Back in the days that film was made, there were no AFTDs, heat-seek security lasers, DNA print scans — and hot currency could still go underground and make up to twenty percent on its street value.

Hogie and his buddies, their problem was, they never read the papers.

While all the smart money was in comp scams, hacking payrolls, bogus cred transfer, forged plastic, Hogie and his buddies went right ahead with the heist. One of the guys broke into the bank manager's home after the old man had left for work, held the wife at gunpoint, got her to ring him at the office, read out the instructions he had printed on a piece of paper. The bank manager's instructions were to locate two guys in grey suits, carrying brown valises and waiting over by the foreign exchange counter, escort them through to the vault and, when the time-lock sprang at ten-thirty, help them fill the valises with as many five hundred dollar bills as the valises would hold. If he refused to comply, played the hero, raised the alarm, his wife would be shot dead.

The plan went okay right up until the phone call. The reason it fell apart after that was because the bank manager wasn't in his office to take the phone call. He was in his limo, nineteen year old trainee called Solitude, from credit control, tucked up against his shoulder, heading for a motel out at Long Beach. If he had taken the call, likely he would have said: 'Go right ahead, shoot the fuckin' bitch.'

The guy holding the bank manager's wife hostage took off straight away leaving the wife to nurse a broken marriage. The two guys standing around in grey suits and carrying brown valises were eventually approached by security and gunned down when they made a break for it. Hogie Corcoran was outside in the getaway car with the engine running. He was still sitting there when the cops arrived and put the collar on him.

That was the heist.

But, it wasn't the heist, or the conviction, that gave Hogie Corcoran his five minutes of fame back in Fifty-One. What gave Hogie his headline space in the nationals, a slot on the Kate Goodyear coast-to-coast late night talk show, and his ugly mug featured on the cover of Time Magazine was the sentence handed down by the Circuit Judge. Twenty-Five years SOPS. A precedent in Californian — also US — legal history. The technomedics called it Organ Senility Acceleration, and explained it away to the layman as controlled white corpuscle deprivation. The politicos, always looking for this year's euphemism, went for Soft Option Penal Servitude — SOPS. Soft option was just how Hogie Corcoran saw it and he was with the politicos all the way. Four hours locked in on an intravenous drip at the Californian Penal Authorities Corrective Medic Center in Oakland sure beat all hell out of twenty-five years hard time in the Federal Pen — maybe eighteen with good behaviour — looking out for your ass and cleaning the needles with con-brewed White Lightning.

So what if, after the medics were through with you, and accounting for any future rejuve treatment, organ transplant, immunity restructuring, you were now twenty-five years short of your natural span on this earth.

That was tomorrow.

And tomorrow — especially with Hogie in the frame — anything could happen.

The bar Hogie drove us to was the Las Vegas Beach on Sunset. The Las Vegas Beach had started out as an upscale fern bar catering for out-of-town tourists who liked their drinks in tall glasses with crushed ice, fruit slices and enough fresh herbs to leave the impression they were sucking on a house plant. The walls were decorated with murals, copies of originals painted before the Big One of Ninety-Seven, showing California falling into the ocean and Nevada cleaning up on the relocated tourist industry. It was one more bright idea for a bar that had faded right along with the decor. These days the bar prices had dropped enough to attract local trade and business was okay. Local trade liked its drinks straight up, no ice, no chaser, no complications.

On the Strip life was complicated enough already.

Hogie curbed the Buick in a parking slot across from the bar. It was one-thirty-five p.m.. Schoolgirl hookers were already out looking for lunchtime trade or, if this wasn't their lucky day, a starring role in a snuff movie. None of them approached us as we crossed the Strip. It was like that when you hung out with Hogie Corcoran. We took a table at the back concealed from the sidewalk by the angle of the bar. Estelle Scriven was sat waiting for us nursing an empty glass.

'I'll stand you a drink, Estelle,' I said, 'but you've got some explaining to do.'

She had her hair pinned up in a bun, round her neck a slender gold chain and a heart shaped locket. Fresh white sweat-shirt against olive skin, jeans and sneakers. I was looking to get mad at her but it wasn't going to be easy.

The bar-keep came round to take our orders. He had a leather apron, two days growth on his face, and a complexion the colour of nuclear rubble. I asked for three bourbons, straight up. What we got was Wild Turkey.

'Finish that,' I told Hogie, 'then go lose the Buick. It's an even bet Craig Homer made the licence plate.'

'Make no difference, Charley,' Hogie said. 'The wheels are hot. Picked it up on a company lot on Melrose this a.m.'

'Dump it, anyway. Put it back where you found it. Anyplace, but park it legal. We don't want the cops running a comp check where it isn't necessary. Estelle and I will be here a while, so don't hurry back, yeah?'

After Hogie was gone I ordered two more bourbons and told the bar-keep to leave the bottle. Then I waited while Estelle worked out what bait she was going to need this time around to play me for a sap. She sipped her drink, taking in the barflies perched in a row on their stools, the bar-keep moving in slo-mo to serve a table over at the window, the AC fan rotating slowly over our heads, moving the fug around but sending it nowhere.

Eventually, she started.

'I was living on the East Coast when I met Danny,' she said. 'He was just out of college. Much younger than me, but that was never a problem. He was trained as a micro-technologist, already had a job with Tsunami Intercontinental, debugging life-support systems. It was love, Charley. The real thing. We moved into a New Jersey apartment, got married, decided against kids till we knew for sure where we were going to settle. I had a job through a friend ran an uptown Manhattan gallery, reception work, typing, filing, nothing fancy. Danny was making good money. We were having a ball. When Danny was seconded to government work on survival capsules for the Moon Base Project we just knew it was going to lead to bigger and better things. What it led to was the Pennsylvania Project...'

'And this is where the MD Factor, and Ross Helgstrom, come into the picture?'

'The MD Factor, sure. Ross Helgstrom, he comes later.'

A pack of *vatos locos* interrupted conversation for a while as they pavement parked their Hogs, pushed into the bar slapping leather, and put their feet up all over the furniture. The bar-keep took them a pitcher of beer and some glasses for while they waited on their women to get through working the Strip. Their heritage was Native American, Spanish Conquistador, and revolutionary Mexican. It was hard to believe, watching them sitting there. Now, they had no place left to go, except back to the *barrio*.

I poured Estelle another drink. She looked like she could do with it.

Then she continued.

'Danny and me, we had a real good relationship. Very physical, you know what I mean?'

I knew exactly what she meant but wasn't about to dwell on it with her sat there looking as good as she did.

'We never had any secrets from one another, not until the Pennsylvania Project came up. Danny was vetted. I was vetted. Danny had to sign all kinds of government paperwork relating to restricted information. Sure, the money was great; we started talking about buying a spread out-of-town, closer to where he worked at the lab, but suddenly he wasn't bringing his work home with him, sharing his problems like he used to. A barrier came down. He took to stopping off at the neighbourhood bar on the way home, "Just to unwind a little, honey," he used to say. Wasn't long before he was bringing a bottle back with him, sitting up late watching crap on the TV, finishing the bottle.'

She broke off, close to tears.

'I was losing him, Charley, and there didn't seem a damn thing I could do about it.'

I reached across and offered her my hand.

She squeezed it once.

Tight.

Then withdrew her hand.

'Was I weak, Charley?'

'Don't make it harder than it already is,' I said.

Estelle had a way of puckering up her mouth on the left, then nodding her head to the right. When she had her hair down it was a vivacious gesture. Pinned up, like now, the movement was petulant...

Dismissive.

I don't think she even realised she was doing it.

'He was falling apart right in front of me, Charley. Whatever it was he was involved in, it was destroying him.'

'Did destroy him, Estelle,' I said. 'And you and me both, we're next in line.'

'After Danny was killed... after the melt-down...'

'You came out West chasing ghosts. Why, Estelle?'

'I needed it to make sense.'

'Losing somebody close, is that ever meant to make sense?'

Estelle sat on that one.

I needed to fill the silence.

'It was all over the papers, Estelle,' I said. 'The Pennsylvania Project set up to create a black hole in a controlled laboratory environment. Bunch of guys out to grab a handful of deep space only it blew up in their faces. Six hundred people died, Estelle, what made Danny so special?'

'You wouldn't understand, Charley,' Estelle said. 'Not in a million years.'

'Try me.'

'August Nine, Eighty-Four.'

'The date of the explosion.'

'Early hours of the morning. Around one-fifteen.'

'Where is this heading, Estelle?'

'Danny wasn't there, Charley. He was home with me. Left for the lab in the morning, usual time, we never checked out the news that early. That was the last time I saw him.'

'Estelle, you told me...'

'The official line, Charley. His name was posted right along with the other five hundred and ninety-nine casualties.'

'His name was on the duty roster for that night?'

'Not till after the melt-down.'

'You realised you might be in danger yourself?'

'I was out of there, Charley.'

'What did he tell you, Estelle. About the project. What was it eating his pride?'

Estelle poured herself another drink.

It was a small one.

'It was a Friday night, two weeks before the explosion. Danny came home late but he wasn't drunk and he didn't have a bottle with him. We went out to a local Chinese because Danny thought the apartment might be bugged. He talked me through the MD Factor experiments, what they were working on at the Pennsylvania Project... critical point at which molecular density reverts to anti-matter, creates a black hole.'

'Last guy told me all this, he ended up dead, too, Estelle.'

'Morale out at the plant was low, Charley. Nobody working on the project, the scientists, the technos, none of them thought it made any sense. The black hole project, they could live with that. But then the politicos hit them with the hidden agenda, attempt to arrest the inversion process, create miniaturisation. The research scientists told them they were crazy, that it couldn't be done, but the State Department kept throwing dollars at them. Then they started moving in their people, taking over the top floor, a white-collar circus, Danny called it. Think tanks, quangos, you name it, all working on the ramifications of a breakthrough the scientists assured them wasn't going to happen.'

'Non-voluntary Zero-cred Relocation Program?'

'That was one of the domestic implementations they were looking at, Charley.'

'So the tabloid smear was for real?'

'Only it was too crazy for anybody to believe. Then the story got revived in the *LA Island Post* and I came out here...'

'And found a property scam?'

'The editor on *The Post* led me, through Hogie, to Ross Helgstrom, only he had already flown the coop. That's when I connected with you, Charley.'

'What did Ross Helgstrom have on the editor at *The Post* that he could get him to print the stories?'

'Nothing, Charley, outside of a fat cred balance. The editor's name was Jerome McCrae. First time I went to see him, he threw me out of the office. Then he calls me up, asks me to meet him at the parking lot out on Ocean Front Walk, Santa Monica. He's sat waiting for me in his limo with a bullet wound in the chest, only he's not anxious to go looking for a medic. Jerome McCrae had had it up to here with himself... with life.'

Hogie Corcoran pushed his way in through the swing-doors of the bar. One of the *vatos locos* locked eyes with him, thought better of it, and went back to carving his initials in the table-top with a switch-blade. The bar-keep had switched on the vusac and four topless girls were dancing on top of the bar. It was an ancient holo. The girl on the end, you could see right through her.

'Just when the dust is starting to settle, Ross Helgstrom comes along and stirs it all up again.'

'This is political dynamite, Charley.'

'You think I don't know that?'

Hogie had reached our table.

'Hogie,' I said. 'Go find us another automobile. One with decent tread and after-burn. We got a long drive ahead of us.'

Then I found the bar phone and put in a call to Smoky Griscom.

Chapter Twelve

The Institute of Primordial Correctness had been good to Smoky Griscom. Good enough to provide him with twenty-five acres of Cucamonga Wilderness carved out of the slopes of Lone Pine Canyon, above San Bernardino, in the High Sierras. The house was Swiss Alpine Chalet style, set in rolling meadowland, with white water cascading down from the redwood slopes to the North, and, to the West, the snow-capped peaks of Sugar Mountain filling the sky and, every evening, putting on a spectacular show as the sun dipped below the tall horizon. Smoky's place was all dark cedar, red brick, fancy balconies, and more tied lace-curtained windows than you could count at a glance.

It was chocolate box.

Fairy-tale.

A long and winding road from Smoky's curriculum that advocated growling over raw prime cuts and building body funk in order to get laid by some good-time post-rejuve divorcee with time on her hands, a gold cred inheritance stacking interest with the First National, and a penchant for ripe meat.

But, what the hell?

Did the chairman of General Motors drive a Pinto?

Smoky shared the house with No-Cherry. It wasn't her actual name but the closest anybody ever came to a correct pronunciation. No-Cherry had appeared after a business trip Smoky had taken to the Far East. Smoky's story was that he had rescued her from the Bangkok child prostitution racket, paid her old man top dollar. But then Smoky always did tell a good story. No-Cherry was twenty-five now, built like a frond, with short silk-black hair, and the complexion of a mocha cream shake.

They were both waiting for us as Hogie Corcoran pulled the four-wheel drive off the dirt track and parked up alongside Smoky's Rolls Expat. Scorched rubber mingled with the aroma of damp soil and moist vegetation. The sun was already down beyond the peaks, creating a pink landscape against a vermilion sky. The air was cold and clean, sharp as fresh squeezed lime over crushed ice. The cathedral silence was unnatural to a native Los Angelino and I cut it with the introductions. Inside there was a meal waiting. Home cooking, No-Cherry-style: beef in gravy stock with coconut milk, rice, chillis that could melt teeth, the works. No-Cherry could rustle up a lean steak and hash brownies as good as anybody else but this was an occasion. Her and Smoky didn't often get visitors out in Lone Pine Canyon.

After we were through eating, Hogie made his farewells and headed back down into the basin to lose the wheels.

'Watch your back, Hogie,' I said.

'I can take care of myself, Charley.'

With Hogie Corcoran, you knew he meant it.

I helped Smoky stack the dishes then we joined the women in the lounge area. There was a wood burner stove, ceramic tiled, with a hammered copper hood that reached up between the support beams of the high ceiling. The stove was centrally placed and dominated the arrangement of the room. A set of open-slatted pine stairs led up to a gallery that surrounded the lounge on three sides, with bedrooms leading off the gallery. It was hard to believe we were only two hours out of LA Island City. Smoky loaded some more logs into the burner and we spent the evening cracking bottles, smoking through a pack of Heaven's Door, with Smoky never once asking why me and Estelle needed to be holed up out in the wilderness.

I liked that about Smoky.

He never asked questions.

Period.

I had explained the set up to Estelle on the drive out from the basin. Smoky had bought the place seven years back from a military man, Commander-in-Chief, Field Marshal Richard D Layard, then military adviser to the US Overseas Forces in Europe. At risk from terrorist reprisal, Layard's property had been protected with a network of heat-seek laser AFTD's and an eight man armed security team working an eight hour roster, four on, four off. Accepting the possibility that not all terrorists out there might have been informed of the Commander-in-Chief's change of address and, wishing to avoid potential embarrassment, the State Department Treasury Office had agreed to underwrite continuance of the security arrangements as a condition of purchase.

Maybe it was the thought of all that military funded security out there in the darkness that put Estelle in a relaxed frame but, around eleven-thirty, she was looking ready for bed.

Smoky showed us to our rooms.

They were adjoining.

With en-suite everything, you name it.

'I owe you, Smoky,' I said.

'You owe me shit, Charley.'

I used the bedroom phone to call Malloy at the Santa Monica Precinct House. Detective Third Grade Theo Lipztic caught the call.

'Theo,' I said. 'It would be good we could get together sometime.'

'I know what you're thinking, Case, but you're wrong. Time I got down to Beverly with the medics you were long gone.'

'You expect me to believe that?'

'I don't *give* a fuck.'

Theo Lipztic hung-up on me so I called Malloy on his home number, in Maywood, and caught him half-way through a suppertime slice of homemade blueberry pie and whipped cream.

I could hear one of his kids screaming in the background and the TV was on loud, tuned to one of those game shows where the contestants come on in seizure and work on up from there.

'Don't say I didn't warn you, Charley.'

'Sure, you warned me, Patrick.'

'When Coombe-Lately came up classified…'

'We're talking history, here…'

'Yeah, and pretty soon you're going to be history, too, Charley.'

'I want you to run a "worm" through the department comp for me, Patrick.'

'Charley!'

'State Department Project, code access *NIMROD*. Pennsylvania research plant blew up in Eighty-Four. I need to know how many employees were involved in the project in total. How the shifts were organised. How many staff would be on duty any one time. Can you do that for me, Patrick?'
'We go back a long way, Charley.'
'That's why you have to do this for me.'
'That's why I should categorically not be doing this for you.'
'But you will anyway?'
'That's not a promise.' He took a bite of blueberry pie.
'Charley, you didn't ask me yet if we found Helgstrom.'
I waited while he got through eating.
I didn't say anything.
He was going to tell me anyway.
'Ross Helgstrom's body turned up this morning at his sister's apartment in Riverside. Her old man, Otis Creek, found him when he came home to pick up a black suit for his wife's funeral. Ballistics matched the slugs they took out of him with the one they found in his sister, Daisy. They dug another slug out of the wall of the apartment found to be bearing residual body materials that matched Daisy Creek's DNA print. Helgstrom and his sister were killed at the same time and in the same place, Charley. Then Daisy Creek's body was moved to Helgstrom's apartment to make it look like Helgstrom was on the lam from the cops.'
'That doesn't make sense, Patrick,' I said. 'Forty-eight hours back Helgstrom made a half-assed attempt to splash me with his pet Rottweiler. The Fed's are on my back because they're after Helgstrom, too, and they figure he'll come at me again.'
'According to the ME, Helgstrom had been dead four days when Otis Creek found him. Charley, whoever it was set you up to apartment sit, it wasn't Helgstrom. Either that or you were talking to a dead man. Who is it behind all this, Charley?'
On the TV the game show was coming to its cacophonic climax. Malloy's kid had quit screaming.
'Do I win the star prize if I get this one right, Patrick?'
'No, but you just might get to stay alive.'
Later, after a shower set to Dead Sea Salts followed up with a shampoo and hot rinse, I crawled into bed. Smoky had promised to set me up with some fresh clothes that fitted in the morning.

Despite my conversation with Malloy, I was feeling in better shape than I had felt for days. I felt better still when I heard Estelle pad across the darkened room and slide in beside me.

'Who was it you were talking to on the phone, Charley?'

'I thought you needed some sleep.'

'You know how it goes,' she said. 'You sit up all evening in front of the TV, can't keep your eyes open. Soon as you hit the sack...'

'It's been a long time since I spent an evening sat in front of a TV.'

'It's been a long time since I slept with a man, Charley.'

I started in slow and easy, taking my time, but Estelle didn't want that. She eased away, straddled me, and I left her to set the pace. It was quickly over. When she came she cried out her husband's name. I held her tight but she still wasn't able to hold back the tears.

'Soon as you hit the sack...'

She had said.

You're wide awake.

Estelle's breathing had settled into a relaxed steady rhythm. I stared into the darkness, Ross Helgstrom, the whole damn mess, barnstorming around my brain like a prairie twister. I'd never even met the guy. And now, according to Malloy, I never would. A third party had entered the frame. A third party — or parties — who had gunned down Ross Helgstrom and his kid sister, Daisy Creek. Maybe Jake Landsaker, too. The complications spread through my system like a Duke's C carcinoma fanning out from the lymph nodes. It was too late for major surgery and, with the garrote the Feds had made of my purse strings, Von Hausen's miracle cure, DN Angel, was a non-viable option. It was only a matter of time before the medics whispered amongst themselves, put on a fixed smile, and sent me home to die. Estelle murmured in her sleep. I rolled away from her and dug my head into the pillow. The dead don't run, Patrick, I thought...

The dead don't need an alibi.

When I woke up it was still dark but there was moon-light enough from the open window to see the figure standing by the bed wearing a wet suit and an empty spring-release shoulder holster. The Colt Cremator that went with the spring-release shoulder holster was in her hand.

'Commander Coombe-Lately.'

'You're not on the payroll, you don't have to call me that.'

I sat up but the nightmare wouldn't go away.

'How the fuck you get in here?'

'Grumann canoe, Charley, aluminium body. Came in on the white water, confused all hell out of the heat-seeks. Thermoselect on the suit set to zero, just in case. You're lucky I'm not a jealous guy, Charley.'

'What about the security guards?'

'I didn't run into them yet.'

Estelle stirred.

Sat up.

Travesty Coombe-Lately placed the muzzle of the Colt Cremator between her breasts and squeezed the trigger. Estelle fell back without a sound.

My move was too slow and too late.

The muzzle of the Colt burnt a ring of fire against my temple.

'It will be a lot easier, you can make it out of here on your own two feet, Charley.'

'I don't get the big splash right here and now?'

'That's Craig Homer's directive not mine. You want to hang on here and discuss it with him, he'll be along anytime.'

'What's your angle on this?'

'Get dressed, Charley.'

I did like she said. When I reached for my jacket, hanging heavy across a chair, she said, 'Forget the hardware, Charley.'

We were down the stairs, halfway across the lounge area, when the lights went on and Smoky Griscom was leaning over the balcony, his bedroom door open behind him. Travesty flat-palmed me away from her, swung the Colt Cremator, and shot him in the chest.

'Jesus, Travesty!'

Smoky slumped against the guard-rail then fell heavily to the floor.

'Keep moving, Charley,' Travesty said.

Out in the hall she found a cupboard that housed the security controls. There was an immediate response button and she pressed it. Then she doused the lights and waited by the front door, one hand on the handle. The two security guys came up the steps like they wanted to be heard all the way back down in

San Bernardino. Travesty pulled open the door as they hit the top step. I saw her arm and the Colt Cremator silhouetted against the beam of their Mag-lights as she swept them away with one arching delayed charge. 'You got nowhere to run, Charley, remember that,' she said, and sidestepped out through the door into the shadow of the porch. Somebody was running across the lawn. Deadwood was splintering in the redwoods to the right of the house. Then silence. From inside the house No-Cherry started screaming, 'Char-lee! Char-lee!' The two guys out on the lawn exchanged whispers. That was when Travesty opened fire. A white laser beam of lightning pointed them out in the darkness. One of the guys cried out as he fell.

Travesty turned, gun held double-fisted, covering me.

'It's set to stun, Charley. I'd have told you sooner you might have made some dumb play.'

'You expect me to believe that?'

'I can prove it,' she said.

And squeezed the trigger.

Chapter Thirteen

A wooden fan was turning lazy circles above the bed. There were cracks in the ceiling, paint peeling in on itself. The paintwork was cream, started out white. Beside the bed there was a bamboo table with a glass top and two bamboo chairs. The carpet was an ornate tapestry of faded dragons breathing moth-eaten fire. There was a window with the shades drawn and an archway with beaded curtains. Beyond the beaded curtains somebody was taking a shower. The bed-linen next to me had been pulled back but was still warm.

The room told me nothing.

Self-select holo decor.

Like you would find in any hotel room, any-place, around the world.

The wall-mounted telephone above the bed started ringing. When I reached for the receiver a medicine ball hit me in the chest. The pain contracted into a muscular cramp that was bearable. I grunted into the mouthpiece.

'Room Two-O-Nine?'

The voice was young, female, and reassuringly Southern Californian.

'Will you be taking breakfast in your room, sir?'

'If it's that time of day.'

'Sir?'

'I'll be down in a while.'

'Breakfast in the dining room is finished, sir. Staff are preparing the tables for lunch.'

'In that case I'll be down for lunch.'

'Lunch doesn't start serving till twelve noon, sir.'
'Okay, honey, you win.'
'I'm not your "honey", sir.'
'I can believe that.'
'Stereotypical and condescending.'
'I liked it better with the "sir".'
'And madam?'
'I guess she'll be taking breakfast up here, too.'
'Thank you, sir.'
And broke connection.

I was tired of 'Old Cairo' and flicked through the bedside holo-control console till I found 'London Savoy'. Travesty Coombe-Lately emerged from the shower as the bead curtains turned into olive-green drapes. She had a bath towel tied in a turban around her head and the body of a ballet dancer. As she crossed over to the bed she left wet prints in the thick pile of the Wilton carpet.

'How do you feel, Charley?'
'Okay, till I try breathing.'
'Residual effect of violent muscular contraction. I had to do it, Charley. We had a long drive ahead and I didn't want you trying anything stupid could get us both killed.'
'Ross Helgstrom is dead. There's a Fed XPD out on me — why are you still watching my ass?'
'The XPD directive is with Craig Homer. I'm working a covert brief that he knows nothing about. This one goes all the way to the Oval Office, Charley.'
'Nimrod?'
'In one, Charley. It was all getting out of hand for a while back there. The State Department had funded a multi-million dollar budget to set up what they called a Conceptualisation and Implementation Program. Military and Domestic were in there competing for a slice of the action. Big Government had no intimate knowledge of any of the ideas that were being mooted.'
'Zero-cred relocation program?'
'You get that from Estelle Scriven?'
'Her old man was a micro-technologist, specialising in survival units. It's what got him killed.'
'That was an accident.'
'Was it, Travesty?'

Travesty unwound the turban from her hair and tossed the towel across a winged chair. She sat down on the edge of the bed. Her body was still damp from the shower. I had to be crazy, the thought that came into my head.

Not now, Charley.

Not with this woman.

'Handled the right way,' she said, 'this could still bring down the Presidency.'

'The right way?'

'Depends which side of the fence you sit.'

'Politics doesn't interest me, Travesty,' I said. 'All I want is out.'

I rolled off the bed, went over to the window and pulled the drapes. The street below was on a steep incline. There was a row of strip joints with a bookshop sandwiched in the middle. An old guy was selling dim sum from a barrow on the sidewalk. The cars were parked tail out.

'Why the fuck are we in Frisco, Travesty?'

'Isn't it as good a place as any, Charley?'

'As good a place as any for what?'

'For what you've had in mind ever since I climbed out of the shower.'

'Don't kid yourself, Travesty.'

'Who's kidding who, Charley?'

Room service came and went but neither of us had any interest in breakfast. Travesty was as good as she looked...

And then some.

'You'd have made a great hooker,' I said.

'Are you talking dirty, or is that just the kind of dumb-assed comment I would have expected you to make?'

After a while it got to be too late for lunch and we both slept. When I woke up Travesty was dressing. Denim shirt, jeans, sneakers.

Functional.

'Where do we go from here, Travesty?'

'Don't get serious on me, Charley.'

'You know that isn't what I meant.'

She pulled a pad and pen out of her shoulder bag and wrote down an address. 'This will find you Jake Landsaker, Charley.'

'You didn't know he was dead?'

'Wrong. Clem Roelof, his driver, is dead. Jake Landsaker was in the Chevy Dominator you saw taking off in the other direction. He was running scared, hoping to cover his tracks, especially after what Estelle Scriven had to tell him.'

'Estelle?'

'Sure, Estelle. You have a problem with that?'

'Not in the way you think.'

'She ran him down following up on the Helgstrom press leaks to *The Post*. They spent a cosy weekend together down at Laguna Beach, buying pottery, checking out the local art. She got nothing out of Landsaker, what could she have got? Landsaker didn't know anything. But he got plenty out of her, like Helgstrom had set him up for the realty scam, like the whole thing had backfired badly and the Fed's were involved. That's when he decided to lay the scam off on his partner, Sam Houseman, and go undercover.'

Jake Landsaker...

I remembered him saying, 'Picture this, Charley... a smart office on Beverly Drive, a good looking secretary who goes down on me once a week, regular as clockwork, despite I'm a fat, ugly bastard.'

And Estelle:

'It's been a long time since I slept with a man, Charley.'

'You have a problem with that?'

Maybe I did.

'There's one thing I can't buy, Travesty,' I said.

'One thing, Charley?'

'Ross Helgstrom... the stories he was feeding the press to support the scam. I can't believe it was coincidence he hit on the truth.'

Travesty had both sneakers on and laced.

'He was fed the script, Charley. The scam was an elaborate cover up and additional payment for services rendered.'

'Did you kill Helgstrom...?'

'...and his sister, Daisy? You already asked me that one, Charley.'

'So who did?'

'Ask Jake Landsaker when you catch up with him.'

She was at the door blowing me a kiss.

'What about Craig Homer?'

'He's just a kid, Charley. You don't think you can handle him?'
Then she was gone.
I took a shower.
Big brass faucets.
Round ivory inlays.
Hot.
Cold.
I stayed under the water a long time. As hard and hot as I could take it. Then I ran it cold till I was blue and shivering. After that I towelled down, grabbed a Jack Daniels from the hospitality bar, flicked through the holo-control console till I found 'Hawaiian Beach'. It was all straw mats, straw mattress, and potted palms. Over at the window the projection made a half-assed attempt at golden sands, rolling waves, and off-shore coral but Hawaii hadn't looked like that for a long time now. I switched off the holo.
It was regular Holiday Inn.
I felt at home enough to ring down to reception.
'How may I help you, sir?'
It sounded like the same girl I spoke to earlier.
'My luggage was stolen at the airport coming in. I need a full kit, medium to large, thirty-six waist.'
'Shoes?'
'I'll stick with what I have.'
'Did it ever occur to you, sir?'
'What?'
'The one of two measurements you can rely on a man knowing is his waist.'
The same girl.
'And I need a rental. To drop off in LAI.'
'Any particular make, sir?'
'You choose, honey,' I said, and hung up.
While I was waiting for the clothes I put through a call to Hetty O'Hara at the West Hollywood Precinct House. Wolfgang 'Wolf' Stacey caught the call in the detectives' squad room.
'She's out on a catch, Charley. Ten-ninety-six. Bar on Lexington. You know what a ten-ninety-six is, Charley?'
'Sure, I know what a ten-ninety-six is, Wolfgang,' I said. 'ten-ninety-six is a mental subject. Means Hetty could be out picking up just about anybody lives in LA Island City.'

'Guy laser-cut a bar-keep for serving up Budweiser instead of Michelob, can you believe that? It was my woman out on the street I'd be real concerned.'

'Yeah, well it's not your woman, Wolfgang. Just give her my regards, will you, only don't get too carried away delivering the message.'

'Dozen red roses to follow, Charley?'

I hung up as the bell-hop knocked on the door with my clothes. Everything was fine apart from the jacket. Tartan check, double breasted, single vent. I handed back the jacket.

'This is your tip, kid.'

Down at the bar I discovered I was in the Hillcrest, top of Van Ness. The bar-keep slid a large bourbon down the bar and I took a table over by one of the bay windows. There were plenty of tourists, South American and Japanese, coming in and out, none of them with kids. Over in an alcove a middle-aged guy was whispering sweet nothings to his secretary. Across the highway Big Zim was still serving up hamburgers like he'd dreamed of when he was fighting on the beaches of Anzio all those years ago. Down Van Ness I could see the Bay and Alcatraz Island. Beyond that, Strawberry Point reaching out into the bay. It was five-fifteen and Van Ness was congested with the kind of small automobiles San Franciscan's love to drive. A Ford Fedora Fast-Back pulled into the hotel forecourt. It was pale pink with fur-lined upholstery. I didn't need to wait for the call over the intercom.

The girl at the desk was wearing a grey suit, long sequinned hair, green tortoise-shell glasses.

'Your keys, sir.'

'You have great taste, lady.'

'We like to tailor our service to suit the customer, sir.'

I settled the bill and left.

Two days from now — if I was still alive — I would probably come up with one of those replies you always wished you'd thought of at the time.

Maybe I could send her a cable.

On the corner a news-vendor was selling the evening edition of the *Bay City Journal*. Before climbing into the Fedora I went over and bought a copy. There was a banner headline that read: 'CUCAMONGA WILDERNESS MASSACRE'. There were also two pictures, one of me and one of Smoky Griscom. Neither of the photographs were anything to write home about. The caption underneath mine said, 'SOUGHT BY POLICE'. Under Smoky's it read, 'MILLIONAIRE MURDER VICTIM'.

The story went on to say how Smoky Griscom, millionaire founder of the Institute of Primordial Correctness, had been found brutally slain at his home in Lone Pine Canyon earlier this morning. Four estate security guards, whose names have been withheld pending notification of their families, were also slain in this savage and apparently motiveless assault. All five victims died as a result of gunshot wounds. Charles Case, private investigator from Century City, LA Island, believed to have been an overnight guest at the house, is being sought by the San Bernardino police Department in the hope that he may be able to assist them with their enquiries.

There was no mention of No-Cherry.

Or Estelle Scriven.

Chapter Fourteen

The Ford Fedora Fast-Back drove better than it looked, holding the curves of the 101 overpass out of San Francisco, tread meshed to macadam, as I built revs towards V-2, heading South for the coastal road and the dying sun. Manual shift was smooth, and the two-by-two turbo-boost block wasn't complaining as I held the gas pedal at ground zero, set the AC to cold, and tuned in a Cajun station — Tommy McClain singing his old hit, 'Before I Grow Too Old'. San Francisco never had been my favourite city. Despite the clapboard houses, the cable car, the fresh abalone you could pick up from the street traders off Fisherman's Wharf on a Sunday morning. Geo-scientists had worked out that the city was creeping towards Alaska at the rate of two inches every year. In forty-seven million years it would arrive, and already the native San Franciscans were complaining about the cold.

In an hour I was free of local traffic, covering a hundred and fifty miles of low-rise urban development, San José and the Santa Clara Valley, before taking the Route One intersection, skirting the Monterey Peninsular, and building elevation towards the coastal range of Santa Lucia and Big Sur.

I was running.

No place to hide, on empty, you name it.

Jake Landsaker was out there somewhere, smiling his fat, ugly smile.

Smoky had stepped into his dead man's shoes.

Nothing was real.

Only the high whine from under the hood, and the winding two-lane ribbon cutting a hairpin contour between the redwood slopes and the white spume and black rock of the ocean below.

I pulled over for gas at a filling station opposite the Visterama Camper Park at Big Sur Point. There was a guy with his head buried under the hood of a Dodge Pick-Up. I sounded the horn and waited. The guy took his time, not about to be impressed by any high-flyers up from the valley. He was about seven-six, two-fifty pounds, with a full beard, red satin cap, and a beer gut left his manhood a childhood memory. The filling station was a Terrible Herbst. Maybe they had named the chain after this guy. He came over smiling, wiping his hands on a rag, taking in the pink coachwork and fur trim.

I hit the button for the driver's window.

'Don't bother,' I said. 'I already heard them all.'

'Mister, I don't doubt you have.'

I got out to stretch my legs while he filled the tank, checked the oil and coolant, cleaned bugs off the windscreen. A hundred yards of empty two lane black top reached out in either direction, sandwiched between the hairpins like a spring release mechanism. Mist was rolling in from the ocean, unseen beyond and eight hundred feet below the camper park. Patches sat on the highway, breaking up the continuity of the single white line. Over in the camper park complaining kids were being washed ready for bed. There was the clatter of dishes and barbecue smoke hung in the mist like smoke signals run out of things to say. Back down the highway, to the North, I heard the low growl of a high powered automobile shifting through the changes as he made the curves of the preceding valley. The growl pumped into a roar as the limo broke cover around the headland. The red Ferrari Berlinetta Berserko took the stretch of mist shrouded highway like an electric current passing through a multi-core cable, tyre tread tearing chunks out of the road as he hit the airbrakes and dived into the next valley.

The grease-monkey was standing beside me.

'Sheee-it!'

'And some,' I said. 'Down the road I'm gonna find that guy buried in the radiator of a Winnebago.'

'Not that baby, no-sir-ee.'

The Ferrari was audible again, climbing up out of the other side of the valley, eating the steep gradient with a succession of deep-throated growls as the driver shifted down through the gears. Then it rounded the next headland leaving us in the darkening landscape with only the sounds of the tourists across the way and the soft tick of cooling metal beneath the hood of the Fedora. On the slope above the filling station a hawk broke from the cover of the conifers, it's wings spread, searching out an up-current. A single high-pitched cry reverberated across the peaks. Darkness came down, infiltrating the mist, like the whole wide world was drifting into unconsciousness.

'Take care, you hear, mister. This road's a mean bastard, especially at night.'

In my rear-view mirror I saw the lights go on in his office and then I was round the next bend, brights carving a tunnel of light through the grey mist, driving to the limit, my mind focused on nothing, except staying alive. Boozoo Chavis was on the radio. 'Lost the Paper In My Shoe'. The lyric didn't make any sense. Tangled conifer root reached down towards the highway, colourless in the beam of my headlights. Outcrops of bedrock inviting me to swerve the wheel, put an end to the whole damn mess in a fireball of twisted metal. A lone biker locked beams with me, hurtling in the opposite direction. We both dipped the brights, grateful for the company.

It was two hours, but felt like forever, before I hit Nepethne, and pulled into the car park cut into the granite beneath the bar. There were seven other cars in the parking lot. One of them was the Ferrari Berlinetta Berserko with steam rising from the hood and from the wheel hubs. The Nepethne Bar had been designed by a disciple of Frank Lloyd Wright. Redwood, cedar beam, glass. Through a geological freak it had survived the Big One of Ninety-Seven. I felt on solid ground. I sat awhile, then climbed the wide paved steps to the bright lights of the bar, the empty wilderness out there lost to the warmth of company, the reassuring clink of ice on glass. At the open charcoal burner a young guy in a white apron and chef's hat was turning burgers. There were two couples and a party of four in the dining area, along with a tired businessman giving the waiter a hard time over the cheese board. The waiter was explaining that the European War of Unification was making supplies a little difficult right now, but the businessman hadn't got where he was listening to other people's problems. Another group was seated in the bar area. Smart dressed kids, up from the Santa Clara Valley, sucking weird drinks through long straws out of tall frosted glasses. At the bar were a couple of big guys in check shirts and denims, pretending to be mountain men. Next to them, perched on a bar stool, was Craig Homer.

'What can I get you, Mr Case?'

'You didn't do your research?'

Craig Homer turned to the bar-keep. 'Large Jack Daniels, straight up, *Cerveza* to chase.'

'So, okay,' I said. 'I'm impressed.'

I parked up on the bar stool next to him. One of the mountain guys glanced over his shoulder then went back to discussing wild hog with his buddy.

'I didn't figure you for a tourist, Mr Case.'

'We all need a break, Craig,' I said. 'Thought I'd come out here, check out if the whales are blowing. Only it got dark before I expected.'

Craig Homer was wearing a tan suit and red sweat-shirt. There was an ugly bruise on his cheek from where I took him with the Winchester Pump. He was drinking creamed coffee.

'Whales come through here in the Spring,' he said. 'By now they're all in the Gulf of California.'

'We have a spring in Southern California? I never noticed.'

'You never noticed a lot of things, Mr Case.'

I drank some of the Jack Daniels and flamed a Heaven's Door. The bar-keep came back over. 'Sorry, sir. This is a no smoking area.'

'Aren't we just a little out of touch,' I said. 'Didn't you hear, the Big C went out with Van Hausen's miracle cure?'

'Nevertheless…'

'Do like the guy says, bub.'

That was one of the mountain men.

Craig Homer smiled.

'What do you think?'

'I think I want a quiet drink,' I said, handing the lighted cigarette to the bar-keep. 'Here, bud. Stick that where you want.'

All of a sudden the bar wasn't such a friendly haven and I was looking forward to getting back on the open road. Just me and the Fedora, pink, with fur trim.

The mountain man had sat back down.

'There's somebody would like to meet you,' Craig Homer said.

'I'm in the book. Have him call me.'

'Don't make this difficult, Mr Case. We are talking about a man of considerable influence.'

'Yeah, who is this guy?'

'I don't have clearance…'

'Can he raise the dead?'

'…to divulge …'

'Can he bring back Smoky Griscom?'

'He can prevent you joining him.'

I stared at him.

'What do you say, Charley?'

'I'm still "Mr Case" to you, kid.'

The mountain man was back. His buddy, too.

We both ignored them.

'You should know,' Craig Homer said. 'Estelle Scriven is okay.'

'You think I give a shit?'

'The way you two guys…'

Craig Homer shrugged.

My mind was on Laguna Beach, local turned pottery, and Jake Landsaker.

'You read it wrong, Craig.'

'Don't I know you from someplace?'

That was the mountain man.

He didn't look like a guy could read, but who needed to read with my mug-shot splashed all over page one of the evening edition?

'I'm in the movies. Walk on stuff. Nothing special. This here is my minder, Craig.'

Craig nodded, the smile back on his face.

'I don't go to the movies.'

'You should, it could broaden your outlook.'

'Say again, mister.'

One of the kids at the table said, 'Hey, lighten up, you guys.'

Mountain Man wasn't in the mood to do that. This was shaping up to be the most interesting thing that had happened to him since he'd seen a surf-boarder taken by a great white off Big Sur Point.

'Butt out, gnat-piss,' he said to the kid.

'I don't mind company, but we're just trying for a private conversation here.'

A placatory gesture.

Knowing any other time or place it would have been the wrong move. A sign of weakness leading to just exactly what I wanted to avoid. But not here.

Not now.

Mountain Man was looking from me to Craig Homer.

'He doesn't look much, but don't let that fool you.'

Craig went for a different approach.

'Go fuck your grandmother,' he said.

'Shit for breath,' I added.

Craig Homer read the head butt before Mountain Man realised that was what he ought to do, grabbing him by the balls and hauling upwards.

The guy screamed.

His buddy was all gut and no guts. Afraid of making the first move, he was left with no move to make. I straight jabbed him in the stomach, putting a twist in the fist as it landed. He sat down on the floor. I was ready with my foot but it wasn't necessary. The guy was happy where he was.

The other guy had come back and had Craig Homer in a full-nelson with his feet six inches off the floor. I hadn't been in a bar-room brawl since I was a kid. It felt good.

Mindless.

Perfect.

Craig Homer had broken free of the head-lock and was about to execute a move, palm flat, his hand a knife-edge. A bad-assed move way beyond what the situation called for.

I gave it all to him.

My fist collided with his head.

A roundhouse that left me nursing knuckle.

'Okay, mister. Cool it, yeah?' Mountain Man said. The young guy in the white apron and chef's hat was advancing from behind the charcoal burner, a carving fork in his hand, leaving the ambrosia burgers to burn. The bar-keep was on the phone to the police. The tired businessman was still complaining about the cheese.

The nearest cops were in Gorda, fifteen miles down Route One towards San Louis Obispo. Fifteen twisting miles of ravine and long lonely drop into the Pacific Ocean. I was in no hurry as I grabbed a bowl of sugar from one of the dining tables.

Brown sugar.

Taste the cane…

Down in the car park, using a screwdriver from a tool kit I found in the trunk of the Fedora, I jemmied the petrol cap of the Ferrari Berlinetta Berserko and dumped the sugar into the gas tank.

Eight miles down Highway One I passed a black and white heading in the opposite direction.

Lights flashing.

Siren wailing.

Like there was anyone out there…

To see.

Or hear.

Chapter Fifteen

It was after midnight when I dropped out of the coastal range, descending through a series of switchback curves — past San Simeon, where William Randolph Hearst built his Xanadu — and rejoined Route 101 on the San Luis Obispo By-Pass. You ever spent time in San Luis Obispo, you'll be grateful the City Council built that by-pass. Thirty-five minutes on auto-cruise took me into Santa Barbara. I pulled over on Cabrillo and parked between the palms and the ocean. I hit the button for the window and could smell the jacaranda. Down on the beach some kids had a bonfire going. Somebody was picking out chords on a guitar. In the darkness beyond the bonfire I could hear waves slapping the shoreline.

Slow and easy.
Like everything else about Santa Barbara.
If you were 'old' money.
And your face fitted.

Santa Barbara had the only stretch of South facing coast in California. With the Santa Ynez Mountains to the north shielding it from high winds, rough seas, and the fog pushing down from San Francisco, the township could boast a climate just like the Côte d'Azur before the Mediterranean died and the European War of Unification turned a ghost resort into a scorched total exclusion battle zone. During the day, on this stretch of coast, you could watch renegade missiles, out from Vandenberg Air Force Base, wandering drunkenly across the clear blue sky before self-destructing over the ocean. Whenever this happened the *Santa Barbara Gazette* would run a headline that read:

'MISSILE TEST GIVES VIEWERS STUNNING SHOW'. To the North, at Point Mugu, the United States Navy was still intent on blasting the offshore island of San Miguel out of the Pacific Ocean.

Nothing bad ever happened in Santa Barbara.

It was just a matter of how you looked at it.

Across the highway the Lazy Swell Motel was advertising vacancies. A billboard showed a kingsize waterbed, its surface rippled, the silhouette of a surfer riding the waves.

I secured the Fedora and crossed the strip.

In the motel office window was a hand-printed notice: 'No blacks, Hispanics, screenwriters, Los Angelinos — Period!'

The author of the notice was sat behind his desk watching an old John Wayne movie on a portable TV. It was called *The Hellfighters*. He was wearing red and blue striped suspenders over a button-up sweat shirt. Between his teeth was a stubbed out King Edward cigar. At forty-seven cents for a five-pack he could afford to use them to splash roaches.

'The bar's closed, mister,' he said.

'Can I get a bottle of JD and maybe a club sandwich for my room?'

'The food we have to send out for. There'll be a surcharge. Besides, you don't *have* a room.'

'Do I get to sign the register or you want a blood test?'

'You a Los Angelino?'

I was tired, hungry, and thirsty enough not to reach over the counter and bust his face. 'Put me down as a Quaker out of Salt Lake City. I'll pay over the rate for the room, you get to pocket the small change... and I promise, not a word to City Council.'

He tossed me a key.

'One-o-six, mister, and you carry your own baggage.'

Room 106 was at the far end of the building with a single window that overlooked the coast highway and wouldn't close properly. There was a queen-size waterbed, sand in the carpet, and rings on the surface of the dresser from where previous occupants had parked their drinks. The girl who arrived with the liquor and club sandwich was wearing roller-blades and had crinoline for a hairstyle. She asked if I required any additional services and I told her, no, I was just dandy. The club sandwich was triple-deck, tuna mayonnaise on every level, no onion, no ground pepper. I washed out a tooth mug, poured a splash of bourbon, and called Hetty on her Venice Beach number. A guy with a New York accent picked up the phone. He wanted to know who the hell I was calling this time of the morning. Usual polite New York style. I told him I was Hetty's private medical consultant and needed to talk to her urgently on a matter of some delicacy and, by the way, could I have his details, too, just for the record.

'That wasn't funny, Charley,' Hetty said, when she came on the line.

'Neither is having a guy answer your telephone at two o'clock in the morning.'

'I was starting to feel like a widow.'

'Well, you should have waited till after the funeral.'

'The way I hear it a day or two either way isn't going to make much difference. Malloy's been on to me, said if you got in touch to tell you to contact him.'

'What can Patrick do — except hand me over to the San Bernardino Police Department. Anyways, the APB out on me is the least of my problems right now.'

'What have you got yourself into, Charley?'

'Hetty, I just called to let you know I was okay.'

'What if I don't believe you?'

'Then that doesn't leave a lot to say.'

'Right, Charley.'

Neither of us wanted to leave it there, hanging on to a line that was deader than a disconnection.

'I'm real sorry about Smoky, Charley,' Hetty said.

'Me, too,' I said, and hung up.

I refilled the tooth mug, ate the tuna club, and crawled into bed. Sleep doesn't come easy on a waterbed, with every restless turn making waves that come rolling right back to haunt you.

The phone bell woke me at eight-forty-five.

It was the desk clerk.

'Mister, I'll have to assume you want the room another day, you're not out of there by nine-thirty.' Starting in just like he had left off the night before.

'Tell me the cleaning staff need to get in and I'll laugh in your face.'

'Laugh all you want, mister. I don't make the rules.'
'Small mercies.'
'Huh?'
'Where do I get a decent breakfast around here?'
'No place I can think of. 101 is right out front. It leads straight out of town.'

The phone was on the way back to it's cradle when he added: 'Incidentally, there's a guy on his way out to your chalet. Smells like a cop, looks like a breed. Or, maybe, it's the other way around.'

He thought that was funny.

'Breed?'

'You know, like one of those Apache bastards rips off the tourists up in the San Bernardinos.'

'You've been watching too many John Wayne movies, bud.'

Down on State Street and De La Gurerra there was a civic statue, in bronze, of a black bull. The bull was called Duke. It didn't look anything like John Wayne, but it would have been great to hang this guy up by it's horns, all the same. Santa Barbara had a Court House, mock Spanish-Moorish style, that didn't look anything like a Court House, either. And trash cans, with ceramic inlaid tiles, that didn't look like trash cans. But, for all the fancy wrought-ironwork, mosaics and towers of the Court House, the circuit judge still handed out two strikes and out life stretches, or a one way trip to San Quentin and the pay-off popper — especially you happened to be hispanic, black, or Los Angelino.

And the trash cans still carried trash.

Detective First Grade Patrick Malloy didn't bother to knock.

Just pushed in through the door.

Took a look around.

'This place is a dump, Charley.'

'No kidding? How did you find me, Patrick?'

'Put a trace on Hetty's line. Figured you'd make contact.'

'So, where's your shadow, Theo Lipztic?'

'I'm on my own time, Charley.'

'You mind waiting while I take a shower, get dressed?'

'Be my guest, Charley,' Malloy said.

We found a beachfront eatery that served decent eggs easy-over, hash browns and links. Down on the sand, local kids were doing freaky things with their bodies. A bunch of middle-aged women were star-jumping to a holo workout instructor. Surfers, out on the water, were making opening incisions in the waves, waiting for the big one. The sun was already high over Santa Cruz Island.

'This could cost me my badge, Charley,' Patrick said. The plates had been cleared away. We were drinking coffee.

'I'm grateful, Patrick. But there's nothing you can do to help.'

'Try me.'

'Well, you could let me have your piece. I can hardly go waltz into a gun shop with a Police Department APB in circulation.'

'You know I can't do that, Charley.'

'Because I'm a murder one suspect?'

'You get apprehended "in possession", the arresting officers are just as likely to gun you down, no question.'

'Then trace the firearm back to you?'

'Charley, I'm here, aren't I?'

The waiter came by with a refill. He was young, short hair, all gym muscle and black singlet. Most occupations in Santa Barbara, you needed a screen-test before you made the first interview. Only beautiful people need apply. Unless you were an Hispanic. Then you worked out of sight, keeping the wheels turning and the streets clean, maybe picked up a few dollars in your pay-packet at the end of the week — if you were lucky, surfacing every once in a while as a cigar-store *Mejicanos* whenever Santa Barbara threw one of its 'Old Spanish Days' fiestas.

'That was a lousy thing to say, Patrick, I'm sorry.' Detective First Grade Patrick Malloy had coal black eyes and a beak for a nose. His skin was olive, his hair shoulder-length and slicked back. He leaned back, pushing his chair up onto two legs. 'That information you asked me to get — you still want to hear it?'

'Sure, I want to hear it, shoot.'

'Pennsylvania Project. Employed one thousand, two-eighty personnel. That's the whole show. At the plant itself there were six hundred staff — scientists, technos, maintenance, clerical back-up — all with maximum security clearance. It was a round the clock operation, eight hour shifts, eight on, sixteen off.'

'At any one time there would be two hundred personnel at the plant?'

'It doesn't take a mathematician, Charley.'

'So, how come the State Department release posted six hundred casualties?'

Patrick Malloy stuck a filter between his teeth.

He didn't light it.

He never did.

'I'm just a dumb cop, Charley.'

'My ass, you're a dumb cop. You ever stop to ask yourself why you've spent twenty years at the same lousy desk. Why you never made lieutenant's bars, captain, even… fat pension to look forward to when they take you off the street? Buy a camper truck for you and Marlene, go visit Josh and Patch when they settle down, make you a grandfather?'

'Sure, I have. But, you need to talk, go right ahead.'

'You smell garbage, you leave it out for collection, Patrick.'

'That simple?'

'This one goes all the way up the hill, and there's not one damn thing you can do to help me.'

Out in the parking lot Malloy gave me his gun. It was a Police Department regulation issue Armstrong Variable. Minimum setting you could flame a straight. Maximum, you could burn a dime sized hole through Valencia Dam at a thousand yards.

I opened the door of the Fedora.

The interior was like an oven.

'Thanks, Patrick, I'll see you get it back.'

Malloy smiled.

Don't make promises you can't keep.'

I wasn't comfortable with that.

Malloy smiling.

Chapter Sixteen

Montecito, in the foothills of the San Rafael Mountains, overlooking Santa Barbara, was a hillside Park Avenue. 'Quiet Money', residing behind Italian-stone walls and imported wrought-iron gates, security low profile, but don't let that fool you. 'Quiet Money' that had resided here since before the quake of Nineteen Twenty-Five, when Santa Barbara had been reduced to a heap of scree at the foot of the mountain, and the City Fathers had orchestrated the rebuilding, creating an Hispanic-style fantasy — Mexican Adobe, Andalusian Farmhouse, Mediterranean Baroque, Castilian Nostalgic, and Moorish Italian — before having to do it all over again after the Big One of Ninety-Seven. 'Quiet Money', that could remember when one of the very last Republican presidents of the United States, Ronald Reagan, lived up in the hills on his ranch, *Ranchos Dos Cielos*, or Two Skies Ranch, with his wife, Nancy, and a black bull called Duke. Could remember their grandparents saying, after the invasion of 'Loud Money' Hollywood movie stars in the late nineteen hundreds, 'I like going to the movies, but I don't expect the movies to come to me.' Could condone their security gunning down house intruders, not because they were black, but because they were Angelinos.

Nothing in the whole wide world could talk louder than 'Quiet Money'...

I parked up on Alameda Padre Salinas. The address Travesty Coombe-Lately had given me had no number. They didn't have numbers on Alameda Padre Salinas. Beyond the stone wall was a stand of sugar pine, branches weighed down with giant cones.

Along the grass verge whip-like ocotillo's bore orange blossom. It wasn't an area Jake Landsaker could afford to live, not even if he was riding high on a realty scam funded by the State Department Treasury. Two kids came by on cycles. A heavy set guy followed up on a bike with more gears than sense and a UV Scattergun hanging loose on a strap over his shoulder. As he went past he took his time looking into the car. I stared right back but it didn't worry him any.

The black and whites rolled up five minutes later. Two of them, one from either end of the avenue, converging on the Fedora, kissing fender front and back. A cop emerged from each patrol car leaving his driver behind the wheel. The young cop was fat, sweat on his brow, circles spreading from under his armpits, staining his navy shirt. His buddy from the other car was older, wiry, his sunburned face cracked like a delta mud flat at low tide. He was holding an Armstrong Variable extended at arms length. His partner settled for wiping his brow, other hand resting on his quick-release holster.

I kept both hands on the wheel, where the cops could see them, knowing better than to make a move that could be misinterpreted.

'Out!'

That was the older cop.

I got out of the Fedora, turned and spread my legs, arms out, hands resting palm down on the roof of the car. The younger cop kicked my feet further apart.

'You done this before.'

Statement, not a question.

'I've seen it in the movies.'

'What's your business in this area, sir?'

The older cop.

He frisked me and dug out Patrick's Armstrong Variable and my billfold. He pulled my ID from the wallet and handed it to the fat cop. 'Go check this out, Tab.' Tab ambled back to his patrol car, passed my ID to the driver who fed it into the dash comp. The older cop had stepped back two paces, his handgun extended. 'This is a regulation issue Police Department fire-arm, sir.' He held out Patrick's Variable. 'Can you explain how it came to be in your possession?'

'Would it make any difference?'

Tab shouted from the patrol car. 'Hey, Ralph, there's an APB out on this guy. Multiple homicide, Cucamonga.'

The guy with the mountain bike and the UV scatter-gun had cycled back up the hill to check out the action. 'Ralph, Tab,' he greeted the two cops.

'Harv,' the fat cop said.

His partner nodded.

'Got us a live one here,' he said.

'Murder one suspect,' Tab said, 'that shooting up at Cucamonga?'

'Angelino?'

'You guessed it.'

'Smog shit!'

That was Harv talking to me.

The older cop cuffed me.

Tight.

'Go easy,' I said, 'it's not as bad as it looks.'

'Can you believe the guy,' Harv said. 'Guns down five people and it's not as bad as it looks.'

I was the only one noticed the gunmetal grey Cadillac Contessa, six doors, smoked windows, as it glided towards us.

The older cop, Ralph, was hustling me towards the black and white when it pulled up along-side. Four burly guys, grey suits, button collars, mirror shades, came out of the limousine simultaneously. Harv tried to get the UV scattergun from off his shoulder. One of the suits gut-punched him and grabbed the Scattergun as Harv went down with his bike. The suit nearest us flashed an ID, up close, in Ralph's face.

'We'll take it from here, officer.'

Ralph squinted at the ID.

'Well, I'll be...'

'Get the cuffs off this man, will you?'

'Who are these guys?' Tab said.

'Butt-out!'

That was the suit standing behind Tab.

'Do like the man says, Tab.'

Ralph found a key and uncuffed me.

The suit with the impressive credentials took my arm. 'In the car, Case. Move it.' I climbed in the back, sank into the leather, surrounded by the suits. The driver was all dressed up in peaked cap and gold braiding, an old guy, could just see over the steering wheel. He engaged drive and the Contessa eased forward. A hundred yards down Alameda Padre Salinas he hung a right between some fancy wrought-iron gates. Scrolled into the iron-work was the name of the place, *Hasuenda Del Embeleso*. 'Embeleso' doesn't translate easily into English. Roughly, it means a seductively inviting landscape which, if you get too close, devours you.

It was good to know that somebody around here had a sense of humour.

Chapter Seventeen

The beginning of the end for the Republican Party as a political force in the United States came towards the end of the nineteen hundreds when Ronald Reagan was elected for his first term of office in the White House. At that election only fifty-three percent of the population bothered to vote. Of that fifty-three percent, only 51 per cent voted for Reagan. The Republican 'landslide', endorsed by unexpected victory in the Senate, heralded a 'Mandate for Change' that was supported by only twenty-seven percent of the population.

So much for statistics.

So much for politicians.

What was important was that this new administration, with its hardline overseas policy escalating from isolationism to interventionism, eventually allowed the CIA enough rope to hang itself.

And the Republican Party along with it.

Ever since the Bay of Pigs, Central Intelligence had been under close international scrutiny. Under the Bush Administration there was The Gulf War and the subsequent supply of US-controlled nuclear weaponry to Saddam Hussein. Then, after Bill Clinton's brief and disastrous term of office and the election of right-wing Republican Kenneth Starr, there was the Second Greek Military Coup, the assassination of prominent British left-wing politician, Daniel Evans, which sparked the European War of Unification, the covert support of Japan's fiscal invasion of Australasia, and, finally, Operation Drawbridge, masterminded by the CIA and funded by expat Cuban sugar money, which resulted in the nuclear destruction of Nicaragua. On the domestic front, with the announcement of a new age of prohibition, and the escalating Ghetto Wars, the silent majority found its voice and swept Democrat Michael Mariscone into power in an unprecedented landslide victory. One of his first moves was to initiate the MacCormack Enquiry, of Thirty-One, which resulted in the dissolution of the CIA. Reviled internationally, and discredited by Big Government at home, nobody was shedding any tears...

Except, maybe, for one or two political throwbacks, still liked to think they could tell their field boys from their house boys.

'Senator Geffen, Charley Case. Charley — Senator Geffen,' Craig Homer said, making the introductions.

Hasuenda Del Embeleso was an adobe style ranch-house with low-pitched red tile roofs, earth-tone plaster walls, arched facades, and more wrought-iron work. We were in the lounge. Deep carpet, comfortable chairs, heavy drapes drawn to reveal rolling meadowland and lemon grove. There was a cabinet with a display of guns from the Old West, a wall-mounted Buffalo head with glass staring eyes, a roll-top bureau.

Barry 'Blowtorch' Geffen had been National Security Advisor to the White House at the time of the Nicaraguan crisis. To come back from that was like trying to free-climb the face of El Capitain, Yosemite National Park, wearing roller-blades. Yosemite meant 'grizzly', and maybe Senator Barry 'Blowtorch' Geffen was just that, because he'd made the climb, all the way, one of only two Republicans — the other was Jesse 'Silo' Fairweather, Senator of West Virginia — to have a power platform from which he could voice his disapproval of the Democrat's 'wet nurse' domestic reform policies and 'soft under-belly' tactics in dealing with the Sov's.

'Sit, Mr Case, sit,' Geffen said. 'Craig, maybe you could go find Rikki, have him fix us some drinks.'

Craig Homer had met me at the car.

All smiles.

'How's the Berlinetta, Craig,' I had said. 'Still running smooth?'

'Berlinetta?' he said, 'I don't drive a Berlinetta.'

I guessed the tired businessman, up at Nepethne, had ended the evening with more than the cheese-board to complain about.

'You handle yourself well, Mr Case.'

'Keep it in mind, kid.'

Now, the introductions made, Craig took his cue and went off looking for Rikki.

'A very able operative,' Geffen said.

'I'm still here, he can't be that able.'

'Perhaps to put the emphasis on "here" would be more appropriate.'

'Craig Homer had nothing to do with me being here, Mr Senator.'

Geffen smiled.

'It's quite refreshing, having somebody talk back at me, for a change.'

'Yeah, how about all those guys in the Senate. Just you and Silo Fairweather, the ultimate vaudeville double-act. Besides, before you offer, I'm not interested in any staff job.'

Barry 'Blowtorch' Geffen, like most larger than life characters was a big disappointment in the flesh. He had paid a high price for the extra years the medics had given him. He was an androgynous figure, his complexion pale and alabaster smooth, all those years of experience — joy, fear, heartache, disappointment — cut away by the surgeon's knife, leaving a blank slab, a tombstone waiting on the epitaph. Every syntho-organ devised by the medico-technologists was buried in his body, holding back the night.

The big sleep.

He was wearing a tan three-piece suit, hand-stitched by Pesterre, on Rodeo. The expensive cut didn't disguise his frailty.

'I've been in a minority situation most of my political life, Mr Case. But what you have to remember, the Senate, the House of Representatives, they don't represent the whole picture. Kennedy made that same mistake and look where it got him. Look at it this way. The Democrats threw a party. It has lasted eighty years. Who do you think it is, out in the kitchen, helping themselves to the booze, the fancy food, waiting for the band to pack up, the guests to go home?'

Rikki came in.

He didn't knock.

He knew he was invisible.

He was wearing a white house-coat and thongs. On a tray, he

was carrying brandy in a balloon glass, JD in a tumbler. He handed out the drinks and...

How can you disappear?

When you're invisible?

'Politics doesn't interest me, Senator,' I said.

Geffen held the balloon in his palms, swirling the amber fluid. 'Me neither,' he said. 'But, power...'

'Is politics?'

'No, Mr Case... a straight eight is power. Politics is the monkey wrench you sometimes need to fine tune the carburettor.'

'Monkey wrench? Don't ever set up as a mechanic, Mr Geffen.'

'I fix a lot more than automobiles, Charley.'

'Charley? I was wondering when we would get familiar.'

Geffen was through enjoying guys who talked back.

Party time was over...

'Craig! Get in here!'

Craig came through the door at the double, a Colt Cremator in his hand.

'Dammit, put that thing away,' Geffen said.

Craig Homer stowed his piece.

Stood there, uncertain of his role.

'Craig, tell Mr Case why you off'd Griscom and his security boys.'

The frail old bird...

A hawk riding the up-currents.

Craig swallowed.

'Periphery damage limitation, sir.'

'You hear that, Case? Periphery damage limitation. Doesn't sound much of a reason for your buddy to get himself killed, does it?'

I held back the red.

The mist.

'And the off-duty roster at the Pennsylvania Plant, is that why they had to die, too?'

'It's why they all died.'

'The melt-down?'

'Life is cheap, Mr Case.'

'You too, Geffen.'

He decided the brandy was warm enough.
Took a sip.
'We own the networks, Mr Case,' he said.
'You're losing me, Geffen.'
'It's time to come on out of the kitchen,' he said. 'Tonight, coast to coast, Kate Goodyear will host a show that will bring down this administration. They used to call it "rat fucking".'
'What part do I play in all this?'
'Don't kid yourself you're that important, Mr Case,' he said. 'What I have for you fits in more with your line of work. You're chasing down Jake Landsaker, right?'
I remained silent.
'I would prefer he didn't end up in police custody.'
'In the old-time Hollywood westerns, the sheriff used to tell his posse "you bring this man in dead, I don't want to see any holes in his back".'
'Times change.'
'Yeah, back in those days the bad guys always wore black. You knew where you stood.'
'And nobody ever heard of exit wounds.'
'If I don't play ball?'
'You're on Death Row.'
'Why is Landsaker so important to you?'
'He links with Helgstrom. Helgstrom could be traced back to me.'
'Why don't I just go to the cops, myself?'
It was a stupid question.
I already knew the answer.
'You'll be arraigned on murder one, five counts, and it will stick. You want, I can make a call, have those guys come back up here?'
'I'll pass on that, thanks all the same.'
This was the moment Estelle Scriven made her entrance. She was wearing red chiffon with matching choke, her hair was down and her feet were bare. She was dressed expensive and looked at home around the place.
'Craig,' she nodded.
'Estelle.'
She went over to Geffen and draped her arms around his shoulders. He took a handful of her backside and squeezed,

smiling at me, letting me know just how things stood between himself and Estelle Scriven.

'Bandit with the babes, too, Geffen.'

'Whatever it takes, Charley,' Estelle said. 'Remember I said that.'

'You make me sick to the stomach, Estelle,' I said.

Geffen cut into the fond reunion.

'Craig, why don't you show Mr Case to one of the rooms upstairs, give him some time to think things through.'

As I got up out of my chair Craig Homer sucker-punched me.

I didn't see it coming.

With a sucker punch...

You never did.

Chapter Eighteen

There was a floral quilt. Lace-trimmed pillows. A clock ticking. On the wall above the bed, a folksy hand-embroidered homily, in a wooden frame, that read: 'WE HAVE EVERY RIGHT TO DREAM HEROIC DREAMS'.
    Giltwood framed paintings by Catlin...
    Wyeth.
    Out on the western plain.
    A needle went into my arm.
    A rush of pleasure.
    Gentle hands were loosening my collar.
    'Char-lee, Char-lee!'
    A sharp slap across my face.
    Then another.
    It didn't hurt.
    Nothing hurt.
    There was a prairie that stretched unbroken to the horizon. An ocean of buffalo, the sky above them dark with dust.
    Rolling thunder.
    The dark tide moving towards me.
    The earth shaking...
    Disintegrating.
    An anxious face, 'Char-lee, you must listen. There's no time!'
    No-Cherry.
    I looked around for Smoky. He had an easel set up in the grass, sketching the buffalo. 'I got no beef with buffalo,' he said, threw back his head... laughed... spat into the dust.
    Disappeared behind the darkening cloud.

'I don't want to leave, Char-lee, this is now my home. There is nothing for me to go back to.'

'Save yourself, No-Cherry,' I said.

'I need help, Char-lee!'

'Smoky, he'll take care of you, just like he's always done.'

'He's dead, Char-lee. Dead!'

Thundering hooves dug for purchase in the soft loam of prairie soil. The undulating black tidal wave swept over us.

The sun went out.

I was on my own bed. The phone was ringing.

The VU monitor told me it was Eddy 'The Peep' Lagunda. Reality didn't come any harder than Eddy.

'You'll never guess, Charley.'

I sat up on the edge of the bed.

'Surprise me, Eddy.'

'Levon Lomax.'

'Levon?' I said. Maybe this wasn't reality after all. A parallel world where none of the shit I was starting to remember had actually happened.

'What happened to Jake?'

'Nothing happened to Jake apart from he's suing for divorce.'

'And Levon?'

'Jake's twin brother, Charley, you believe that?'

'No kidding. I've been sat here trying to figure it out since you last called.'

'Business slack, Charley?'

'You know how it goes, Eddy.'

Next it was Malloy's turn.

'You're home.'

'That's a dumb thing to say, Patrick.'

'I tailed you as far as State Street, Charley, then I got dumped on by a bunch of Yale graduates in grey suits.'

'I know the guys you're talking about.'

'Friends like that...'

'You should have stayed out of it.'

'You still have my piece, Charley?'

'No I don't, but I can make a trade. You get to have your picture all over page one of the *LAI Post*, arresting officer in charge, when I bring in Jake Landsaker.'

'Landsaker?'

'Grand larceny, fraud, and murder one on two counts. Daisy Creek and her brother, Ross Helgstrom.'

'Landsaker is dead, Charley.'

'Keep on believing it, Patrick.'

I set the phone to answer, took a shower, and dug some fresh clothes out of the cabinet. After some coffee I fixed myself a late breakfast of tacos, chilli, and refrieds from the freezer. While I was eating, I activated the domestic comp for a print-out on the mid-day edition of the *Post*.

They used to call it 'rat fucking'...

Was how Barry 'Blowtorch' Geffen put it.

'WHITE HOUSE WHITEWASH WON'T WASH' said the headline.

Underneath it read:

'Following Kate Goodyear's sensational exposé on nationwide television last night of the Federal Government's complicity in the bizarre Nimrod project, Congress has stepped up its demands for President Harry Stanton Eldrich to make available all documentation relating to the Administration's highly controversial Zero-Cred Relocation Program. An emergency session, still in progress, has called for an independent enquiry into events leading up to the tragic explosion at the Federal Government's Special Projects Research Establishment in Barryville, Pennsylvania, last fall, which claimed six hundred lives. At the time of the disaster a White House spokesperson had stated the explosion was as a result of an irreversible-mode nuclear meltdown situation. This claim has now been verified as unsubstantiated.

'White House sources have indicated that the President is preparing to address the nation this evening. As yet, there has been no official confirmation from the Oval Office. Informed observers on Capital Hill are openly speculating that the President may use this occasion to announce his resignation from high office. A Washington source is quoted as saying: "We have absolutely no doubt in our minds that what we describe is happening and has been happening in the manner in which we describe it as happening".'

I read that last part again.

Had the world gone crazy...

Or was it just me?

On page two there was a rerun of the Barryville disaster with a photograph of rows of bodies laid out on a baseball pitch. I wondered if one of those bodies was Estelle's husband, Danny Scriven. The page five editorial had a long piece about zero-cred zones, covering the same old ground under a headline: 'THE FINAL SOLUTION?' Nowhere in the paper was there any mention of the MD Factor, laboratory-generated black holes, or miniaturisation. It was a smart move on Senator Barry 'Blowtorch' Geffen's part. With President Harry Stanton Eldrich left to do all the explaining, it wasn't likely his credibility, or presidency, would survive.

The next time the phone rang it was Jake Landsaker.

'You probably think I'm crazy, ringing you like this, Charley.'

'You've got a nerve, I'll give you that.'

My body was shaking free of the narcotics. I felt lousy, my temples ached, my mouth tasted like I was just through siphoning oil from an engine sump.

'It doesn't take nerve,' he said, 'I'm fresh out of options — did you catch the TV last night, see the headlines this morning?'

'A long way from a round of golf at the Marine and County, right, Jake?'

'Too fuckin' right, Charley.'

'And that big production number you put on for my benefit out in the Mohave.'

'I was covering tracks. Wasn't my idea to put the burn on you, too, Charley. That wasn't in the script.'

'The Feds?'

'Who do you think? Only, I had no idea back then.'

'The Rottweiler, that was the Fed's, too?'

'Okay, so it was a dumb play. I was running scared and you nosing around digging for dirt wasn't helping any.'

'Tell me about the scam, Jake.'

'I didn't have any problem with the scam. Ross Helgstrom already wrote the book. After Estelle Scriven put me wise on what was going down I set up some outfits of my own, carried on right where Helgstrom left off, buying up dead acreage at rock bottom prices, selling it on to Landsaker Realty. When the scam looked like blowing I had Paco go in turn over the office, get rid of any paperwork on Helgstrom or the Treasury deal.'

'Leaving Sam Houseman with a pile of bills and a delinquent overdraft.'

'The guy was a mug, Charley.'

'Why did you kill Daisy Creek?'

There was a pause.

'You know about Helgstrom?'

'It doesn't take a genius.'

'His sister, she was no innocent party, Charley. They were in it together.'

'Why'd you call me, Jake?'

Landsaker was one more ugly character in an ugly world. I was through talking to him.

'I want to turn myself in, Charley, before the Feds get to me. I figure with a good attorney, I'll get away with five to fifteen, time off for model prisoner — all that crap. Which is a whole better deal than riding a concrete block at the bottom of Marina Del Rey.'

'What makes you think the Feds can't reach you in the Pen?'

'I'll take out some insurance, lodge all the details with my attorney.'

'Expedite on demise?'

'Yeah, that's what they call it.'

'Won't help you when you're dead, Jake.'

'I won't be dead, Charley. It's a deterrent.'

'The Feds don't know the meaning of the word,' I said. 'Besides, you ever stop to wonder why the Feds should still want you dead with it splashed all over the headlines?'

'What are you telling me?'

'The cops, the Feds, they're the least of your problems. There's another party in the frame, and you know that, because this other party is why you're ringing me, setting me up to get your own fat ass off the hook. Only, what you don't know, Jake, is that same party is going to off you as part of the same scenario. No loose ends, and that way they stay invisible.'

'I don't know what you're talking about, Charley.'

'Central Intelligence is what I'm talking about.'

'Are you crazy! We're talking history here.'

'You're wrong, Jake. What we are talking is you want to play me for a sap, hire me to watch your back, see you safe into police custody. Am I right?'

'Charley!'

'Where are you, Jake?'
'Palm Springs.'
'That's a way out — I'll need some time to get there.'
'You'll come?'
'Sure, I'll come. Give me a time and place.'
'You know Quake City, on East Saturnino? I can be there after eight.'
'Everybody knows Quake City, Jake,' I said. 'I'll be there.'
It was that easy.
Tracking down Jake Landsaker.

The Plymouth Pulsar was parked in my regular bay in the residents' lot in the basement of the building. I slid my plastic into the ignition and the engine fired up straight away, the sub-frame vibrating in that old familiar fashion, as seven out of the straight eight cylinders growled into action.
I released the handbrake, went for manual on the shift. The stick wouldn't budge.
'The fuck...' I said.
The auto-comp cut in.
'Emergency over-ride!' it squawked. 'Activation of drive-select to precipitate terminal malfunction of all systems!'
'The fuck...' I said, again.
Cut the engine.
Climbed out.
Sprang the hood.
I found the device wedged in the pinion bracket of the gear selector. A wad of plastic explosive that would have detonated, under pressure from the gearbox control-rod, as soon as manual drive was selected. Gelignite is easy to make. Any punk-ado off the street could show you how. You take a bowl of nitric acid and toss table tennis balls into the acid until the mixture turns to jelly. After that, all you need is a steady hand and a smooth ride to get to where you are going. It looked amateur — but then any professional will take pride in making a hit look like the work of an amateur.
I had too many enemies out there...
To even think about it.
I closed the hood and took the float up to reception. Harry Cohn, the old security guy, was back at his usual place behind

the desk, asleep, with a mid-day edition of the *Post*, a quarter-pounder with everything, and a can of Michelob in front of him on the desk-top.

'Good to see you, Harry,' I said.

But not loud enough to wake him. Using the phone on his desk, I rang the Sheriff's Office, got through to Tactical Division, gave them the registration of my Pulsar and the location.

Then I called Farouk.

Chapter Nineteen

You couldn't miss Quake City — hammer on hold, cruising the lazy Yucca frond shadows of uptown East Saturnino Boulevard, Palm Springs. Not after the sun had held its own against the roll of the Pacific, bedded down behind the Santa Anas, the evening fresh and cool, the cicadas and road runners catching their breath, the kangaroo rats coming out to play Russian Roulette with the brights along the broken white lines of Route Ten between LA Island City and the State of Arizona.

There was a two acre forecourt with floodlights spread around the perimeter wall. The floodlights focused on a façade of cracked stress-concrete, tumbled masonry, and *trompe-l'oeil* shattered windows. There were jagged gaps in the brickwork of the parapet and a scree of rubble above the entrance canopy. Dry ice pumped from flush-set apertures around the walls. Above the building, a scaled down holo of a Bell Jet Ranger Copter hovered in the desert sky, bathing the area in incandescent light from the Night Sun slung beneath the belly of the copter.

Thirty million candlepower.

Blue white.

Quake City.

A bad taste joke that passed for an upscale restaurant, selling high priced French food to a gold cred clientele, mainly movie people out from the Basin, resting in a bed of synth-oil, supported by high-tensile spring loaded buttresses. The same construction blueprint that was heralded as the ultimate in anti-quake technology and used all over the West Coast before the Big One of Ninety-Seven happened along to prove everybody wrong. The theory was that a building with its foundations resting in a bed of synth-oil and further cushioned by the spring loaded buttresses would be spared the worst effects of any quake. In the event, what happened was: the first tremor fractured the synth-oil basins and the synth-oil leaked away into the earth leaving the buildings, now already unstable, to take the full force of the second shock wave that destroyed the Western Seaboard of the United States, and has gone into the history books as the Big One of Ninety-Seven.

So much for theory.

What the architects who designed Quake City did, they turned the whole idea around on its head. Linked to a comp activated random sequencer, the high-tensile sprung buttresses that supported Quake City could deliver anything up to a force four on the Richter Scale. Nobody knew when it was coming, that was the big attraction. When it was quiet for too long a spell the management over-rode the comp sequencer and activated a quake themselves, just to keep the customers interested. Since the White House had finally pressured the geo-scientists to come up with a permanent solution — substrata electronic scans and a series of pressure release zones along the fault lines — Quake City was the only place in California where you could still get to feel the earth move. Folks loved it, especially when the comp delivered a full scale four, and everybody got to run out of the building without settling their tab.

Bad taste never did hurt a good idea in Southern California. One million two hundred and seventy thousand people, native Californians, marginals, out-of-state tourists, travelling businessmen, illegals, died during the Big One of Ninety-Seven and the three weeks of fire-storm that followed in its wake. There wasn't a one of them, if they were to rise from the dead, wouldn't be happy to be seen eating in a chic joint like Quake City, on East Saturnino Boulevard, Palm Springs.

Farouk parked the Chevy Shuttle in an alleyway one block up from the restaurant. His dipped beam caught a mongoose foraging in the trash cans. It's eyes became pinpricks of laser as it looked in our direction, then dived for the safety of the shadows. A derelict was propped up against the wall singing *One For My Baby* like he thought ol' blue eyes was still alive and well and living in his burnt out body. Farouk secured the vehicle and we walked back along the strip to the restaurant. I stayed out on the forecourt while Farouk went in through the atrium and into the manager's office. I flamed a straight and waited.

It was five minutes before the first shudder hit the building. It wasn't much. Like somebody in deep sleep shaking off a bad dream. The second was more impressive. When the third and final shock wave came, people started running out of the restaurant.

Screaming.

Having one hell of a night out.

I saw Jake Landsaker break free of the scrum around the entrance and hurry across the forecourt to a Camaro Casablanca rag-top. He was wearing a two-piece pale blue satin finish suit, a polka dot cravat tucked into an open-neck polo shirt, snakeskin loafers with brass buckles. Going on the lam hadn't affected Jake Landsaker's dress sense any. I came up to him as he was sliding in behind the wheel, shoved Farouk's Smith & Wesson Firestorm into his face and said, 'Move over, Jake, we already got a driver.'

I waited while Landsaker slid across to the passenger seat, then climbed in the back, placed the Smith & Wesson against the back of his head.

'Hey, Charley, who needs that?'

'Live with it, Jake,' I said.

'We're among friends, right?'

'Don't kid yourself.'

Over by the entrance Farouk was having some trouble with a couple of waiters and a guy in a cummerbund who could have been the manager. Farouk pushed one of the guys and came away fast. I reached over the front seat and leaned on the horn, directing him to us. The guy in the cummerbund was now on the top step, trying to persuade the crowd of diners that the excitement was all over, why didn't they all come back inside, finish their meals, *filets de poisson gratinés à la Parisienne, boeuf à la Catalane, pêches cardinal,* who the fuck cared what it was they were eating before Farouk came in convinced the manager it might be good for his health he set the comp sequencer to manual over-ride and go for a full four on the Richter Scale?

Just so long as they came back inside.

Lightened up.
Settled the bill.
Farouk slid in behind the wheel of the Camaro.
'Triple One?'
'You got it, Farouk,' I said.
Farouk flamed gas, floored the hammer, and rode a four wheel drift out onto East Saturnino, heading east towards the intersection with Triple-One and the main drag back into LA Island City.
'This guy with the Police Department?' Landsaker said.
Farouk took his eyes off the road.
Momentarily.
Looked at Landsaker.
'The fuck is this guy, Charley?'
We wound through the spilt spaghetti curves of the intersection, hit Triple-One and locked beams with six lanes of oncoming traffic. Up ahead, a Porsche 912 was glued to the outside lane. Farouk kissed fender and sounded his horn, giving the guy a shot of brights into his rear-view mirror. The Porsche driver wanted to play, showed us his converging reds, until Farouk stowed rubber, hit jet boost, and carved the Porsche into an inside lane.
'Hey, go easy, will you,' Landsaker said.
I still had the Smith & Wesson Fire-storm against the back of his head but it was the road up ahead, rushing to meet us, that was giving him all the problems.
'You're fuckin' crazy, you know that?'
'You got it wrong, Landsaker,' I said. 'You're the one's crazy around here. Crazy to think we were going to wait around back there for the big set-up.'
'I'm on the level, Charley.'
'Tell it to the cops.'
'You still going to turn me in?'
'Isn't that what you wanted. Good attorney, five to fifteen, early parole with good behaviour?'
'Suppose I told you I changed my mind?'
'Yeah, well, I didn't change mine, Landsaker.'
The Camaro was eating up the highway, spitting it out, deep-fried, through the twin after-burners. Traffic swerved out of our lane to avoid third-degree burns to the coachwork. A few

drivers may have sounded their horns, but the sound never caught us. Up ahead, was the junction with Interstate Ten and the elevated section through San Gorgonio pass, with the San Gorgonio Dam plugging the gap between the San Bernardino and the San Jacinto Mountains.

'Can we talk about this, Charley?'

'You'd be wasting your breath.'

A searing blue-white light engulfed the car.

'Shit!' Farouk said.

An amplified voice boomed out of the night sky:

'*Attention Camaro Casablanca, proceeding on northbound carriageway... This is the LAIPD, Airborne Traffic Control Division... you will cut boost and pull over, I repeat...*'

Farouk retarded the jet boost, pumped gas to compensate, and dropped the treads. The automobile bounced once then held steady. Using the change-down to lose speed, he crossed through the lanes and pulled up on the hard-shoulder.

'Sooner than you thought, Landsaker,' I said.

'Space cadets, that's all we fuckin' need.'

That was Farouk.

The cops of the LAIPD Airborne Division were an untouchable elite, patrolling the four thousand square miles of air-space above LA Island City in their Bell Rangers armed with laser canon and Gatling Supersaturate Solid-States that could fire fifteen hundred rounds of impact-explosive shells for every second the co-pilot or gunnery officer kept his finger on the trigger. The airborne cops had a song they liked to sing at divisional reunion dinners. It went: 'Ashes to ashes, dust to dust, if the laser don't get you, the Gatling must.' Those guys weren't joking. Apart from the firepower, their Bell Rangers were fitted-out with auto-navigational comp scan graphics, for flying blind when the fog came down, on board link-up with Federal Central Comp, Night Sun floodlights, and laser directed surveillance that could monitor and record a conversation between two mute rats half a mile down in the city's sewage network. The only Divisional Headquarters directive these copter-jockeys chose to obey was the order restricting them from ever making touchdown, come face to face with the citizens they were policing, while on active patrol. It was the antithesis of community policing, and democrat Eugene Goizueta had vigorously campaigned to have the

Airborne Division disbanded, or its roll restricted to back-up work for the emergency services. The campaign had cost Goizueta his governorship at the recent State elections. To the average Californian, those kind of liberal ideas were best kept strictly east of the Rockies.

Farouk killed the engine. Overhead, the copter hovered, hidden behind the blinding blue-white light of the Night Sun. I pictured the pilot, busy on the wave band: 'Operations…? Border Rose SWATS negative boost-zone highway contravention… possible ten-twenty-nine… request mobile ground support. Target blue Camaro Casablanca…location, five west Interstate Ten, north carriageway, Route Triple-One… Tag Delta Lima…'

Smoky Hollow accent.

Just like Chuck Yeager.

The one they all used just as soon as they got up there.

It was one hell of an amount of public funding for one lousy speeding ticket.

The black and white pulled off the highway two minutes later. A uniformed cop got out of the driver's side and walked back towards us, taking off his black leather gloves as Farouk hit the button for his window. It was something I had seen in a movie, sometime.

'Farouk?'

The cop was still five yards away, his Colt Cremator coming clear of the holster. In the cold glare of the Night Sun I saw Craig Homer smile as he levelled the weapon. Farouk went for the ignition, but it was too late. A searing white bolt melted windscreen, took him in the head. Jake Landsaker screamed, 'No! Not me. Not me!,' threw his hands up in front of his face in a useless gesture as a second stab of lightning struck the cab of the Camaro. I had the back door open, was rolling down the steep embankment, hit an irrigation channel and crawled forward, away from where I had landed. The Night Sun followed my movement, the pilot of the Bell Ranger losing altitude, trying for a clearer visual confirmation of what was going on on the ground, allowing his gunnery officer a better target.

Ashes to ashes.

Dust to dust.

Craig Homer appeared at the top of the incline, a razor-sharp silhouette in the glare of the Night Sun. Another car drew up, doors opening, shouting. Craig Homer turned round, raised the Colt Cremator, then threw his arms up in the air as a shot punched his chest. It was solid state ordinance and passed straight through his body, creating bloody carnage.

Craig Homer crumpled, rolled down the embankment.

Now there was somebody else on the crest, another sharp-relief silhouette, holding something high above his head towards the glare of the Night Sun.

A police shield.

'Patrick Malloy, Detective First Grade,' Malloy shouted. 'LAIPD, Santa Monica Precinct! Tag three triple two, seven-zero!' Then: 'Don't move an inch, Charley!'

Malloy stayed motionless, his hand holding the badge still raised above his head, praying for Marlene's sake, for Josh and Patch.

Jesus!

For himself, goddammit –

That the on-board Gatling wouldn't open up, spread him like pink mist, lost to the whorls and eddies of tail-drag, out on the highway.

A voice boomed in the sky: *'ID confirmed. Negative make on the black and white. You had us confused some, up here, sir.'*

'Not too confused, thank Christ,' Malloy said.

Amplified laughter echoed in the darkness beyond the Night Sun.

They weren't down here.

Left to organise the body-bags.

'Query further assistance?'

'That's a negative, Captain.'

I climbed the embankment. Malloy's battered black Ford Sedan was there. Detective Third Grade Theo Lipztic was over at the Camaro, running a Mag-light round the interior. The Night Sun cut a crazy circle, then went out. Showtime was over. Out of the darkness the Bell Ranger's navigation beacon lights became visible. Red and blue, converging into a single cold star as the copter disappeared in the direction of San Gorgonio. An automobile went by on the highway, heading for Palm Springs. Others followed. Freeze-framed moments of irreversible violence...

Lost to normalcy.

Theo Lipztic extinguished the Mag.
Walked over.
'Buddies of yours in the Camaro, Case?'
I turned to Malloy.
'Farouk,' I said.
'Farouk? Shit, Charley.'
'Call the medics, will you?'
'You're talking resus' viability, forget it.'
That was Lipztic.
'The other guy?'
'Jake Landsaker.'
'Jake Landsaker?'
'Yeah, Jake Landsaker. You got your headline, Patrick?'
'I'm losing it.'
'You and me both, Patrick. Call the medics, will you?'
'I'm talking to myself here. You want I should draw a picture?'
It felt good hitting Detective Third Grade Theodore Lipztic. It felt so good that, when he didn't fall over the first time, I hit him again.
'I didn't see a thing, Charley,' Malloy said.

Chapter Twenty

I was standing over the freezer cabinet, deciding between the Dirt Farmer's Market Day Special and the Ocean Pie, when Travesty Coombe-Lately waltzed into Fat Ernie's twenty-four hour delicatessen, on the corner of Pier Avenue and Santa Monica Boulevard. She was dressed to kill — bangles, beads, and copper bracelets — hair studded with anti-grav sequins, slow-mo fronds, like seaweed stirring in the low waters of an ebb tide, high stepping gait that a shrink would identify with psychotic tendencies.

Sometimes, even the shrinks got it right.

An old guy was over at the cooked meat counter ordering sliced Boloni. Fat Ernie was on his stool at the check-out, his face buried in a late edition of the *Evening Post*. Above his head there was a sign that read: 'CASH ONLY'. On the front page of the evening edition it said: 'NO COMMENT FROM THE OVAL OFFICE'.

I picked up the Dirt Farmer's Special.

And the Ocean pie.

They were both cold enough to burn my fingers.

'The Nicaraguan nuke-out, that was deliberate, Charley,' Travesty said. 'CIA long term initiative to go covert. They were through with all the media coverage.'

It wasn't easy, choosing. The Dirt Farmer's Special had chuck beef, onions, carrot, potato. The Ocean Pie, abalone, squid, prawns and Trevalli.

'President Eldrich hasn't made his resignation speech, yet, and you want to know why?'

I'd caught an early edition. Somewhere inside, tucked away at the bottom of a page, it had said: 'MILLIONAIRE'S KILLER SLAIN IN POLICE GUN BATTLE!' It had gone on to describe how Detective Patrick Malloy, of the Santa Monica precinct, had shot down delinquent cred bounty hunter Craig Homer, wanted in connection with the murder of Samuel J Griscom at his reclusive Cucamonga Wilderness home two days ago. Homer had died while resisting arrest after being stopped for a traffic violation on Route Triple-One out of Palm Springs. I had never thought of Smoky as having a regular Christian-name. Samuel J... What the hell did the 'J' stand for?

'He has been advised to strike a deal with the Republicans. They don't push for resignation, the Federal Bureau doesn't reveal their complicity in the Nimrod Project.'

'What do you think, Travesty?' I said. 'Dirt Farmer's Special or Ocean Pie?'

There had been no mention of Jake Landsaker.

Or Farouk, sat there decapitated behind the wheel.

Travesty reached behind her, took a can of dry roasted almonds from the shelf, popped the ring-pull, tossed some into her mouth. Fat Ernie looked up from his paper, 'Hey, lady, you didn't pay for the nuts yet.'

'I'll be there,' Travesty said.

I threw the Dirt Farmer's Special back in the freezer unit. 'Why is it, you think, I always end up going for the fish?'

'Geffen is dead, Charley. Estelle Scriven killed him.'

'Whatever it takes, Charley,' she had said.

'Remember I said that.'

'But that's not how it will read in the papers. Tomorrow's headline, Charley: "SENATOR BARRY 'BLOWTORCH' GEFFEN DIES IN TRAGIC AUTOMOBILE ACCIDENT".'

The Ocean Pie had a picture of an old weather-beaten guy, grey beard, big grin on his face.

Looked like Santa Claus after liposuck.

'Recently appointed liaison assistant, Estelle Scriven, also perished in the fireball that consumed the Senator's limousine. She stabbed him a hundred and thirty-seven times, Charley. That's as personal as it gets.'

'A hundred and thirty-seven times?'

That was the old guy with the Boloni on his way over from the cooked meat counter to settle up with Fat Ernie. He took a rye loaf, fresh baked, from the shelf along the aisle, looked back, started laughing. He was still laughing as Fat Ernie took his money, watched him out through the door.

'Neat, huh? You've got to hand it to those guys.'

'Sit the phone, Travesty,' I said, 'maybe they'll make you an offer.'

'And, maybe, I'll accept — I hear the pay's good.'

I went over to Fat Ernie and paid for the Ocean Pie.

It was three-thirty a.m. when I arrived at Hetty O'Hara's place on Ocean Front Walk, Venice. I had the Ocean Pie and a quart of Old Crow in a brown paper bag under my arm. I pressed the buzzer for Hetty's apartment and waited while the securiscan camera gave me the once over, then the front door buzzed open.

It was an old building, no elevator or float shaft, and Hetty lived five floors up, on the top floor. She had a great view of the ocean, but that didn't make the stairs any easier to climb. She was waiting for me on the stairwell as I made the last flight, wearing an old check dressing gown that she only ever wore when she was alone, or in familiar company.

I handed her the brown paper bag.

'The guy's still here, Charley,' she said.

I leaned against the balustrade, looking down into the long dark drop. Long and dark enough for your whole life to pass before your eyes while you were falling.

It was a good enough reason not to jump.

'It's getting like there's nobody left you can trust in this world,' I said.

'Was there ever, Charley?'

'Sure, Hetty,' I said, 'sure there was.'

Fireball

A NOVEL BY
JOHN B SPENCER

Preview

BLOODLINES

Preview of the next Charley Case novel, 'Fireball'...

Chapter One

To all the regular soaks warming a bar stool down at the Maverick Bar — off Venice Front, Santa Monica — Joe English had always been called Joe English, despite his first name wasn't Joe, and his second name wasn't English, either.

The English you could understand, because England was where he hailed from originally. Got up and out of there a few short weeks before the Sov's began lobbing tactical nukes across the English Channel and the European War of Unification spiralled into irreversible nuclear meltdown...

The Joe?

Well, that was anybody's guess.

It was one of those late July afternoons, tread melting in park and only losers and abusers, stranded up there on planet Nothing Hurts, venturing out of the shadows, when I called into the Maverick for a passing hit of Old Crow on the way back through to my apartment in Century City. It was three fifteen p.m. and already a long day. My Plymouth Pulsar was freeloading on two cylinders, my cred status was tightrope-walking the big red ocean, and I'd spent the morning ticking off those hours that remained chasing down a kid with no complexion to speak of and an address that amounted to a sleeping bag and a two room clapboard on the beach at Redondo. The kid came on like a polite pain in the ass, then took me from behind with a baseball bat. I was still hurting and it wasn't just my pride. I'd been looking for a lead on his older sister, just like his parents had paid me to do. It didn't take a private investigator with more broken promises than good sense locked into his tail-drag to appreciate why they weren't interested in the kid brother.

The new guy, chasing roaches from glass to glass behind the bar, was a kid, too.

You get used to it.

'What happened to Henry?'

'Henry?'

'Don't tell me — another funeral.'

Henry had kept bar at the Maverick for close on forty years. He *was* the Maverick.

'Nobody died, far as I know.'

'Shows how much you know, kid.'

The phone saved him coming back for more. He picked it up on the second ring, then turned around, said, 'There a Charley Case here?'

The soaks, who could, guffawed into their drinks.

That's how new the kid was.

I nodded and grabbed the phone.

It was Joe English.

'Thank Christ I found you, Charley.'

'Perfect timing, Joe,' I said. 'Five minutes sooner, ten minutes later, who knows how history might have been changed.'

The kid stood there, listening.

I let it pass.

'This is my one call, Charley. I'm in the holding tank, Santa Monica Precinct House.'

'Then maybe you should be calling a lawyer?'

'Lawyer, I don't need, Charley. Best he could do would be to get me back out on the street, and that's the last place I want to be right now.'

I knew Joe English well enough.

But not that well.

We'd shared a few drinks, traded jokes that were only funny at the right time, wasted some afternoons at Sunningdale, placing bets on also-rans and natural born losers. We got along just fine, but that didn't make me his next of kin. Or the first guy

he would run to in an emergency.
'Why are they holding you, Joe?'
'I don't have time to go into that. You know my place —'
'Off Divisidero — I was there the once, but I doubt you remember.'
'Happy days, Charley.'
'You say so, Joe.'
The Old Crow was gone.
Just a glass, looking for attention.
'You think you could get over there right now? If Cissy's not there —'
'Cissy?'
'You didn't get to meet her, yet. We've been going together a couple of months.'
'Has to be serious.'
'Charley, she's not there, wait till she shows up. Get her to pack a bag, get her out of there.'
'Slow down, Joe,' I said. 'Say she won't up and go on my say so?'
'Just tell her, Bruno was cut loose.'
'Bruno?'
'Yeah, Bruno. Just tell her that.'
The kid still hadn't noticed my empty glass.
'So, where do I take her?'
'Who cares, Charley. Just as long as it's no place Bruno is likely to look. How about your apartment? You have a spare bed she can use?'
'Joe, I hate to bring this up, but —'
'Yeah, I know. I'm not asking any favours, Charley. You'll get paid, whatever the going rate.'
'How long?'
'However long it takes, Charley,' Joe English said, then hung up.
The kid took back the phone.
'There a problem, Mr. Case?'
I looked at my empty glass.
'You mean well, kid, and Charley will do just fine.'
'While we're on the subject, the name's Levon.'
'No offence, but that's an empty glass sat there, and life's too short to be remembering the tag on every guy reached me one from the top shelf.'

Mathias Cockburn.

That was Joe English's real name.

The way he told it, back in England they'd had enough good sense to drop the 'ck', pronounce it 'Coburn'. Over here, any barfly looking to build a laugh and have himself included in on the next round used it for material. After a while the joke went anorexic.

As for the Joe.

That was still anybody's guess.

Joe English lived in a second floor condo, with a balcony designed to take the heat and overlooking a pool that was slick with sun lotion. There was the usual pool-side furniture, and grass coming up through the cracks in the paving.

I expected to see a scriptwriter lying face down in the water...

Telling me his life story.

On the third ring, she pulled the dead-bolts, opened the door. A woman in her early thirties, no tucks you would notice, with mousy brown hair, thin body, wearing Joe's dressing gown, and giving off kinetic energy like you could fry just thinking about touching her. She shouldered past me and leaned over the balcony rail.

'Take a look at that pool. My life, right?'

Her eyes were hazel, soft, like the nut had left the shell too soon, vulnerable and bitter, all at the same time.

I could smell the booze.

Every pore in her slim white body working to sweat it out of her system.

Fighting a losing battle.

'You want an informed opinion, or do I play it for laughs?'

'Watch my face crack, mister.'

'Cissy, right?'

'You have some ID?'

'You think I'm a cop?'

'Don't make me laugh. When was the last time you opened your mouth without a big fat question mark in tow?'

'You don't do so bad, yourself.'

I showed my permit.

'Freelance, huh?'

'That way I don't have to write this all up in triplicate when I get back to the office.'

'You want the car, it's parked out front. Didn't need to come waltzing in here between me and the soaps.'

I checked my watch.

'*Golden Girls*, right?'

She laughed.

'So, okay, you've been there.'

It was my turn to laugh.

A guy in a suit, with a briefcase, crossed the pool area, let himself into a first floor condo directly opposite. His security alarm blipped once.

'Four thirty-five, right?'

She spun on her heel and disappeared back into the shadows of the apartment. When the door didn't slam shut in my face, I followed her through to where she was building another drink at what passed for a wet bar in the lounge — a coffee-table loaded with three empty bourbon bottles, one JD, two Rebel Yell, a quart of Jim Beam that still had a story to tell, and a plastic ice bucket with a finger of lukewarm water sat there at the bottom.

'Some night.'

'You needed to be there,' Cissy said.

She sat down on the sofa, pulling the loose folds of the dressing gown to cover her knees.

'Joe said to tell you Bruno was on the loose.'

Cissy reached for the remote, switched off the television set. The sound had been on low, just a whisper, but still the silence filled the room. If I had been expecting the earth to move, I'd have been disappointed. 'So, how come Joe can't tell me this for himself?' Cissy said.

'Maybe the Los Angeles Island Police Department could answer that one for you.'

'Meaning?'

'Meaning Joe's in jail; don't ask me why, he didn't get round to saying.'

Cissy reached for her drink, then changed her mind. Maybe the earth *had* moved — only I didn't notice.

'Grave-digger,' she said.

'Grave-digger?'

'Bruno's street name.'

'Meaning he buries people?'

'No, meaning he digs them up.' She changed her mind about the drink. 'Listen, ...whatever your name is —'

'Charley, Charley Case.'

'Well, listen, Charley,' she said, 'maybe Joe is involving you in something here you might just as soon walk away from.'

'So, now you got the story of *my* life.'

That got a laugh.

'Just another dumb-fucker out to show how tough he is.'

'I got nothing left to prove, Cissy.'

I looked around the room. It was still identifiable as the place Joe English lived, despite the alcoholic cuckoo he had invited into his nest. The easy-chairs had antimacassars, there were chintzy curtains, a cricket bat and pads displayed on the wall like an heraldic symbol, a Hockney print of some young guy submerged in a pool that was a whole lot cleaner than the one downstairs — you could always trust an expat, especially a Brit, to hang on to most of the reasons he had wanted to leave home in the first place. If Joe was here right now we would be drinking single malt, despite the nearest distillery not to have been nuked into terminal precipitation was as far away as Sydney, Australia. The place stank of booze, over-filled ashtrays, and micro'd refrieds. Whatever Joe English got out of this relationship, it wasn't a little lady he could come home to of an evening.

I was through playing games.

'Look,' I said, 'you ring the Santa Monica Precinct House, check out Joe's there. Then pack a bag, I'll be waiting in the car. The way I understand it, Joe would be a whole lot happier you came over, stayed at my place a while.

'And, another thing,' I added, 'there's going to be some house rules, otherwise this thing don't work out.'

Cissy followed me out to the balcony.

Joe's dressing gown was three sizes too big for her and had given up hanging on to one of her shoulders.

'Don't hold your breath, Charley,' she said.

I sat in the Pulsar, engine running and A/C pumping, for thirty-five minutes. Homebound commuter traffic on Divisidero was building up to terminal malfunction. Sometimes, the parking bays in LA Island City got to seem like they were the fast lane.

For Joe's sake, I went back upstairs, rang the bell another three times, then flat-footed the door.
Cissy was gone.
There was a door, off the kitchenette, leading to a fire escape. It was wide open.

Detective First Grade Patrick Malloy of the Santa Monica Precinct House wasn't pleased to see me. He had been looking forward to an early dinner with Martha and the kids, maybe a picture show with Martha, while Martha's sister, Roseanne, in on a visit while the dust settled from another broken marriage down in Atlanta, Georgia, looked after Patch and Josh, made sure they did their homework, got to bed on time.
'Don't break my heart, Patrick,' I said.
'What do you take me for, Charley? You think I'm that stupid I would try?'
'Just tell me why you're holding him and I'm history.'
'Don't kid yourself — history you learn from.'
'That, I would like to believe.'
Malloy was sat behind his desk in the detective's squad-room on the second floor. There were six other desks, along with a water cooler and a coffee machine, and enough paperwork building up to write a book on how City Hall still liked to keep the average cop from getting on with the job that the honest citizens of Los Angeles Island City assumed their tax contributions were funding him to do. Malloy's desk was over by the only window. He would have had a great view of Santa Monica Boulevard, and Big Joe's Doughnut and Grill across the strip, were it not for the slatted steel security shutters that closed out the sunlight and left Malloy hidden in the shadows beyond his desk lamp, the way brights on a country highway conceal more than they reveal.
'What's your interest in Joe English, Charley?'
'He's my client — as of this afternoon.'
'How come?'
'He called me from the tank, asked me to look out for his old lady.'
'His old lady?'
'Cissy — that's as much as I had.'
'Cissy McLaughlin?'

'You tell me, Patrick.'

Malloy dug a photograph from the pile of paperwork on his desk and flipped it into the lamplight.

'This her?'

It was a head and shoulders shot. Cissy's eyes, at the same time, washed out and highlighted by the tears she was angry to be shedding. They were just as hazel, just as vulnerable, but the bitterness had been replaced by something else...

Resignation.

'Black and white was called to the scene a half-hour back,' Malloy said. 'Slot City, on Wilshire. Sat there in a photo booth with her head blown away. It was a class act, Charley. First two shots, nothing to chose, third print, *Kabloom!*'

I didn't get it.

Didn't want to.

'There in the slot, Charley, three prints. Whoever did this had a great sense of humour.'

'Yeah, Patrick, we all love a clown.'

'Who's complaining? Can you imagine — fixing a positive on what we had left sat there in the booth. Colt Cremator, French kissing, doesn't leave much for Dental Records.'

'We go back a long way, Patrick,' I said. 'Don't say anything will change that.'

Malloy moved his head into the light. Olive complexion, curved blade of a nose casting a long shadow, black hair sleeked back behind his ears; native-born Mescalero Apache — don't get fooled by the name — pebble in his mouth for moisture, taking the only shade this side of the horizon, watching his first white man break cactus, pray for cool clear water, and wondering how much soul he could take from the white man in his dying...

'Your old man has a lot to answer for.'

'You forgive and forget, Charley.'

Patrick Malloy... the *original* Patrick Malloy, big buddy of Patrick's old man before he was born — golf, real estate, car keys on the table of a Saturday night, strictly for swingers, local mayor up at Lake Arrowhead — who else but Billy Gomez, just like one of us, would get the ski franchise? Billy Gomez, special vote of thanks to his benefactor, christens his first born with a name tag that stretches back through ten generations to the isolation dormitory, Ellis Island.

Don't ever mention the Statue of Liberty.
'Forgiving, that's easy, Patrick,' I said. 'Next time you're in over your head off Marina Del Rey, you try forgetting how to swim.'
'He died, Charley. How long do you hold a grudge?'
'Cissy died, too.'
Malloy went back into the shadows.
'I'm sorry, Charley.'
'You and me, both.'
I let out a sigh.
Couldn't help it.
'Somebody better tell Joe.'
Malloy stuck a filter-straight between the blades of his teeth.
I didn't expect him to light it.
He never did.
'He's your client, Char ley,' Malloy said.

'Fireball' will be published in the spring of 1997.

Also available:

Fresh Blood

edited by Mike Ripley & Maxim Jakubowski

"MOVE OVER AGATHA CHRISTIE AND TELL SHERLOCK THE NEWS..."

A landmark anthology featuring the cream of the New Wave of British crime fiction, with a detailed Foreword from Mike Ripley recounting the genesis of the Fresh Blood group of crime-writers, and introductions from each author explaining how their stories came to be written and their attitudes to modern British crime fiction. *Fresh Blood* also includes a story never before published in English from the late Derek Raymond.

Contributions from...

Nicholas Blincoe
John Harvey
Stella Duffy
Russell James
Maxim Jakubowski
Mark Timlin
Ian Rankin
Derek Raymond
Joe Canzius
John B Spencer
Denise Danks
Graeme Gordon
Mike Ripley
Chaz Brenchley

Available Now, price £6.99
ISBN 1 899344 03 9

BLOODLINES